NONCONFORMIST

NONCONFORMIST

JANE PARRY

Published in 2023 by Rosamund Books

Typeset in Times New Roman and GillSans
178pp

ISBN: 9798398325119

When we say that body and mind are connected, this does not mean just your own individual body and mind. In you are all your blood ancestors and also your spiritual ancestors.

— *Fear*, Thich Nhat Hanh

For J and A

I

PROLOGUE

Tyn Llan
2015

When we arrived here, I knew as soon as we got out of the van that there would be two things. The first was that I had already fallen in love with the place, the second was something I had to tell myself out loud, to save myself from the first.

'Oh,' I thought, 'I am going to fall in love with this place. I must be careful not to as I am going to have to leave it at some point, because it is rented.'

I repeated it, acknowledging the one and enforcing the other as I moved things from the van into the house, past the barn with the woody honeysuckle clambering up the wall.

'*Rented.*'

The dining room is small, windowless.

'I feel as though I have been in this room before.'

It is still, quiet, easy to imagine an old woman sitting here, or a man. Easy to dismiss as whimsy.

The decision to move to Anglesey was rushed, taken from the barn in Brittany out of sheer desperation. We did not know the island at all and consulted Google maps to see where on earth we were going. The satellite images that took us to the centre of the island left us none the wiser.

We landed at Trefor crossroads, drove another mile down the road, then another half mile down a track, the brambles screeching in slow motion along the side of the van. The house was on a rocky outcrop, slightly raised above the thicket of blackthorn.

It was secret, private, hidden, green. We loved it – I loved it, and let myself plant onions, painting '*NIONYN*' in white capitals on flat bits of wood. I occasionally re-minded myself of the mantra (love it : rented), which held both the concept of my fervour and the tacit understand-ing that I would not be in this place forever.

I let myself put roots down, walking the triangle between the house, the farm and the church – an eternal triangle that took me up track (dusty / muddy) along road (fast) down path (straight) and across field (lumpy, bog-gy) home.

After a year living at Tyn Llan I discovered that my paternal grandfather grew up next door, at Pentre Bwaau. I had no knowledge of my dad's family history and barely any connection with his family, having lived separately from him since I was about two years old. I had wandered about a bit since then.

Learning that my grandfather had lived in this place instantly strengthened the roots I had already established, going deep down to a powerful sense of belonging.

Pentre Bwaau is most often empty, a handsome holiday home facing south, exposed to the sea wind on all four sides. This is where my dad's dad, my grandfather John ('Jack'), grew up, and his forefathers before him. The only two houses down this track, 'Pentre' and Tyn Llan have a very close relationship; the one is more or less the other. I discovered that I am living in the same place my ancestors lived – that it is the place I come from.

Pentre Bwaau translates as 'Village of the Bows' – it was once an armoury for the Sheriff of Anglesey, whose men fought at the Battle of Bosworth. The house used to be the heart of an industrious community, with a smithy, dairy, laundry, stables and cowshed all positioned around a central well. Now the roof tiles on the cowshed are gone, the beams skeletal against the big sky. The steps to the cowboy's byre rise above a midden of pots and nettles. The ash tree bends to the shape of the stone gable.

The estate sold off the house in the nineteen-fifties, and tore down the ancient smithy in the early noughties. Pentre's new owner was so shocked at this barbarity that she planted trees where the buildings had been, as a remembrance and to see some life there still.

Most of my grandfather's family are buried in Llandrygarn churchyard, right next to Tyn Llan. In the year I had lived here before knowing anything about all this, I had unwittingly passed their graves every time I went to church.

Having been made aware of the connection, I began to sift through digital archives, pore through church transcripts and dust off old headstones. I began to form a strata of dates, a pattern of names.

As I was in the same place they had been, there was this affinity, this poignant link. I walked up and down the lanes and knew the crows were looking at me. Ancestral ravens swooped low overhead.

It was new to me, this old family. It was not that I forgot my maternal spiritual guardians, more that they were joined in some great heavenly club by a body of ancestors from my paternal side – my great-grandfather, my great-great-grandmother and more.

Anecdotes from an elderly great-aunt gave me real stories. I had not actively sought this lady out, rather, Maxie found me.

It was Maxie who pointed at Pentre Bwaau from the window of Tyn Llan. She assumed I knew the history and had chosen to live here because of it. It was Maxie who told me of all these connections, of my great-grandfather John Parry, a tough old buzzard who would pitch out of The Bull into his cart, drawn home by his horse so familiar with the route he took the left turn after Gwyndy automatically, his owner dead drunk in the back.

Maxie – the name conjures up blowsy montages of cosmetics and racy 1960s minis. The real Maxie, whilst I imagine having had her fair share of these, is more suited to her full name, Margaret Grace.

She stands at all of five foot in the hallway at Tyn Llan, flanked on either side by my son and daughter who tower above her like saplings. She looks delighted, her eyes and smile are bright. Formerly the headmistress of a Liverpool school, she remains immaculate. She wears tiny shoes, her step is careful.

She does not dwell on her own experience of living at Pentre – she moved there in the late forties with her mother and sister, after her father died. Three women down a long track, with no car or central heating. It's easy for me to wield the rose-coloured spectacles from the vantage of my twenty-first-century double-glazed home, but the reality must have been terribly difficult.

Maxie's mother – Jane Parry – was my grandfather's

sister. Maxie's fragments of family memory disarmed me – I was absorbed in their story.

I visualised the marriage of my great-great-grandmother in the little church. I had the documents, the signatures and dates, and was living a hundred yards from the very spot, with no close neighbours to disturb my train of thought.

I went to church on Sundays, and walked past the church in the field every day of the week. So it was easy, in a way, to form a picture under the sky, to dramatise their lives. I imagined my grandfather as a sixteen-year-old, heading up the track to the Great War. I put him in a scene with Annie Williams who lived at Tyn Llan then, looking after her parents and handicapped sister.

Annie and John walk up the track together – he has a limp – and she asks him what he will do now, after the War. Their words were the first, and in Welsh. That seemed important.

Annie's two brothers went to another war and sent silk handkerchieves from Egypt. Weirdly, I have them, given as keepsakes by Annie to Maxie, then gifted to me, along with a souvenir trinket pot, *Cymru am Byth* written on the side. I keep my earrings in it and use it every day.

There was more: a thick dun pottery mug with WELSH PEASANTRY painted beneath the scenes of daffodils and hats. Women in unlikely lime green aprons are DRESSING THE GRAVE WITH FLOWERS. The pottery aesthetic is questionable, but this too seems important – a reminder. The pot holds my pencils and computer passwords.

Then there are the photographs. There is Pentre Bwaau in the thirties, showing the long barns and the smithy still standing. Great-grandfather John Parry in his cap and *sbectols*, standing in front of a black Austin.

'He had one of the first cars on Anglesey,' said Maxie. Apparently there is a plaque to him in Amlwch somewhere. He used to drive from Amlwch Port to Pentre Bwaau over Parys Mountain, via the pub in Llannerch-y-medd, in second gear all the way. I can smell the burning clutch from here.

The other photos show him and his wife, Margaret. Older, they are standing in the garden. He wears a cardigan, as all grandfathers must. Hands on hips he looks down at his grandson, barely crawling. Margaret is short, with a weathered face and compact body. They are a lifetime away from their younger, sharper wedding shots at Bangor Cathedral.

There is one photograph of my great-grandmother Margaret which is perhaps my favourite. She is caught in profile, dark cape, shoes, hat, walking up a track of the same tones. The bare branches of the tree behind her are whisked in the wind so that everything – the figure and the landscape – become almost merged into one. I scanned these photos recently. They are old, small and it is difficult to make out details. I zoomed in – and in – to reveal the soft contours of her profile – her mouth, which is mine, and my father's.

All these places – the tree at the gable end of the barn, the track – are still there, identifiable. If you wanted to, you could recreate the same shots a hundred years after the original event. A hundred years, three hundred years – a drop in the ocean. There have been archaeological digs around Pentre that suggest habitation there several thousand years ago.

Inspired by all this, I write about ten thousand words of historical fiction, work it to bits, then tear it up. I can't write fiction and I'm not a historian. It was sweet in its way, placing people at altars, golden hair in the sun, but there was a danger of cloying sentiment, of the stench of death and dates. I was trying to cram the mass of this newly researched information into a text.

'What's the point? They're all dead anyway.'

My children groan when I impart another newly acquired Fascinating Historical Ancestral Detail at any given opportunity. Is there really any purpose in making people aware of how quickly they died –

1 day

11 weeks

5 months

9 months

12 years

18 years

29 years

That long, sad list carved in Roman lettering, set deep within the blue slate covering them in Llandrygarn churchyard. Does it matter what sort of disease took them so ferociously in 1826, or how hollow the coughing sounded in the back bedroom? How is it relevant to us, here, now?

There were the survivors, who lasted into their sixties and seventies. Richard Williams, brother to the children above, died aged ninety-two, making him the 'Old Man of Pentre'.

As I pieced it together I continued to identify with them. There was no avoiding it, as it was carved in stone. Another survivor of that long list was my great-great-grandmother, also called Margaret (they do this to confuse us). Sister to Richard, 'The Old Man of Pentre', she died aged thirty, leaving a one-year-old son – my great-grandfather John Parry (the old buzzard).

Richard (the 'Old Man of Pentre') died a bachelor,

leaving the tenancy of Pentre to his dead sister's son, his nephew John. I worked it out one day, sitting on that tall plinth looking at Margaret's long low grave, close to the church door, with the busy ants and the yellow primroses. John grew into an old buzzard through being a mariner, going to sea at fifteen and saving enough to set himself up at Pentre when his uncle Richard died.

John farmed Pentre and had nine children of his own. His wife Margaret must have taken no shit. Originally from Amlwch, Margaret's dad was a carpenter working on the ships in the busy port there.

The cursive script on her birth certificate shows a large cross instead of a signature: *The Mark of Jane Hughes, Mother.* Like so many then, Margaret's mother was illiterate.

Throughout all this research, there's the church, and there's the chapel. There are schisms and wars and I read around these subjects, sticking my head into hefty tomes on The Welsh Nation, Politics, Identity, Language.

I learn about the invention of the tractor and worry about whether a farm boy would own a bicycle in 1918. I look at published photographs of farm labourers around the same time – what did they wear, what did they farm?

I veer away from the idea of writing fiction towards an accurate historical perspective. Reading *The Rural Poor in Eighteenth Century Wales* should clinch it, I think, but find my heart dries at the statistical factuality of it all, the figures, classifications and certainties – where is the soul?

There is one man who appears in several of these books, who is nearly at the top of my ancestral tree – five great-grandfathers ago, in fact. Wiliam Prichard has a passage in *A History of Nonconformity in Eighteenth Century Wales* and another Welsh-language book is written solely about him.

Maxie gives me this slim yellow volume and I begin to decipher it. The text is set very tight and the Welsh is beyond my limited understanding. She has underlined some words in light pencil, here and there: 'Richard' and '*pastynau*'.

Much of the information for these books was taken from material written by one of Wiliam's sons, and is kept in Bangor University Library Archive. I learn that Wiliam Prichard is acknowledged as one of the founders of the Independent movement on the Isle of Anglesey, Ynys Môn, the 'cradle of nonconformity'.

Great-aunty Maxie is a staunch Nonconformist. As Congregationalists they look after their chapel in a collective way, independent of outside rule. Wiliam Prichard's remains are buried beneath the first chapel, built by him and his fellow Nonconformists in 1748.

The original version would have been of wood and straw, physical evidence of their hard-won right to wor-

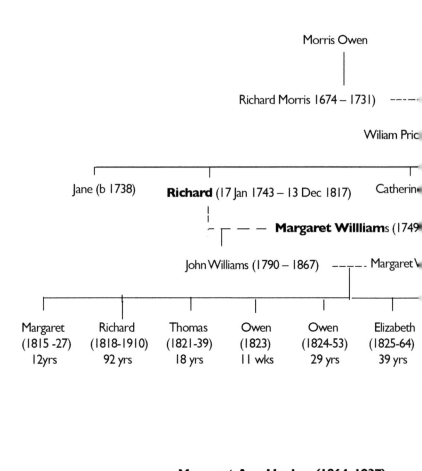

Morris Owen

Richard Morris 1674 – 1731) ----

Wiliam Pric

Jane (b 1738) **Richard** (17 Jan 1743 – 13 Dec 1817) Catherine

Margaret Willliams (1749

John Williams (1790 – 1867) ----- Margaret V

Margaret	Richard	Thomas	Owen	Owen	Elizabeth
(1815 -27)	(1818-1910)	(1821-39)	(1823)	(1824-53)	(1825-64)
12yrs	92 yrs	18 yrs	11 wks	29 yrs	39 yrs

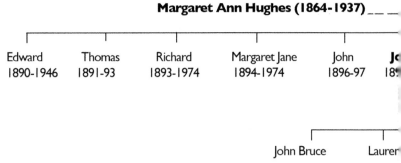

Margaret Ann Hughes (1864-1937) __ __

| Edward | Thomas | Richard | Margaret Jane | John | J |
| 1890-1946 | 1891-93 | 1893-1974 | 1894-1974 | 1896-97 | 18 |

John Bruce Laurer

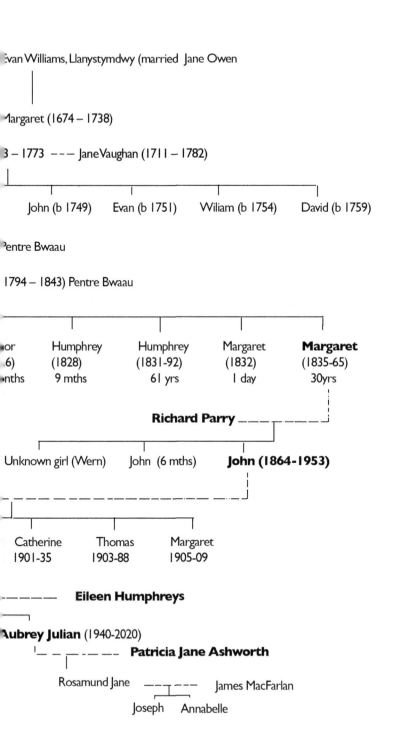

Evan Williams, Llanystymdwy (married Jane Owen

Margaret (1674 – 1738)

3 – 1773 --- Jane Vaughan (1711 – 1782)

| John (b 1749) | Evan (b 1751) | Wiliam (b 1754) | David (b 1759) |

Pentre Bwaau

1794 – 1843) Pentre Bwaau

or	Humphrey	Humphrey	Margaret	**Margaret**
6)	(1828)	(1831-92)	(1832)	(1835-65)
nths	9 mths	61 yrs	1 day	30yrs

Richard Parry _____

| Unknown girl (Wern) | John (6 mths) | **John (1864-1953)** |

| Catherine | Thomas | Margaret |
| 1901-35 | 1903-88 | 1905-09 |

------ **Eileen Humphreys**

Aubrey Julian (1940-2020)

'_ _ _ _.— _ _ **Patricia Jane Ashworth**

Rosamund Jane ---┬--- James MacFarlan

Joseph   Annabelle

Pentre Bwaau circa 1930

John Parry, Pentre Bwaau

Margaret Ann Parry, Pentre Bwaau

Margaret, John and baby Bruce, Pentre Bwaau circa 1935

ship in their own way.

The contemporary building which Maxie attends is painted a pale blue, the interior an unexpected pink.

'I went to a talk about his life once,' Maxie said. 'At the end they asked all those who were related to Wiliam Prichard to stand. Most of the audience got up, though I didn't.'

Through Maxie, I know that I am related to all sorts of people. Here's 'Uncle' Glyn, here's Richard and Owen...a huge network of people. *Perthyn* – to belong. I belong to them, they belong to me – I kind of like that. I can see how it might drive you bananas occasionally, but still, I like that.

My grandfather was first-language Welsh, whereas my dad was prohibited from learning the language. I wanted to find out how Welsh has been all but been eradicated from my family, when it was once so decidedly prevalent.

I am conscious that this is not an individual story – this lost generation of Welsh speakers – but a very common one. In looking primarily at the life of one man I hoped to understand something of the process leading to that loss. I wanted to stick to the facts, but felt some authenticity in interpreting them too.

WILIAM

Llangybi

June 1738

They hold their drinks like armour, tight across their chests. Their skin has a silken sheen and they talk with increasing volume – intense monologues directed at close range. You notice every detail at such proximity – how their faces have puffed a little, their eyes shrunk somehow, their subtle senses rendered obsolete.

The liquor comes in all colours – copper, tan, peat and a gold elixir. The noise of a dozen conversations happen at once, across each other, building to a crescendo of raucous laughter.

From this peak the mood descends, to repeated jokes and sorrowful confessions, sinking to a petulance where grown men are easily offended, quick to anger. Their gloom is lifted by another round, and so the cycle goes, the tide rising and falling as the sun makes its way across a perfect sky.

Outside, Wiliam is at once shamefaced and defiant in the too-bright light. All is in full technicolour – the Llŷn peninsula in high summer.

The earth aches for rain.

He crosses the road and takes the path behind the church, down the field where the sheep stare and scatter. The stream runs along the bottom of the valley and he follows it under the tree canopy, swiping at the hungry flies.

It is four miles home to Glasfrynfawr. Wiliam crosses the bridge and continues along the holloway, the walls encased in moss, the stones bound together by roots of hazel. Dogs bark in the distance and he can hear conversations on the other side, though he cannot see the people through the leaves.

At the beech he lays his hand on the broad trunk and looks up to where the path forks off from the track. He has the choice of two routes here – straight ahead, parallel to the stream, the easy but long way, or the shortcut up over the Garn. He takes the uphill route, the stones piled one on top of another horizontally to form a staircase beneath the branches.

Halfway up Wiliam sits on a clump of rocks on the edge of the copse. The trunks of ash and oak are as mottled as the stones. Some are upturned, ripped from the earth like teeth, the roots clean within the pale brown soil. Wiliam gazes south to the Irish Sea, a couple of miles away. You can see the whole parish from here, a natural hand's span. In the foreground of his view sits a sheep, sphinx-like, facing west. In a field way beyond and below is the silhouette of a horse, next to Capel Helyg, the tangle of headstones a tiny mimicry of the rocks surrounding him, strewn about as if by a giant's hand.

He follows the margin of the wall and as he climbs higher the view pans out. The stones are rounded and white, the hawthorn struck east by the prevailing wind – a spare, familiar landscape. To his back is Cardigan Bay and the promontory of Harlech Castle, but Wiliam's focus is ahead, to the peak of Garn Bentyrch.

At the summit there is a breeze, the earth pales below, the mountains of Llŷn rise like individual dreams. From this vantage point he has a panoramic view – west to the distant line of Ireland, clockwise to the Isle of Anglesey, the yellow sand of Llanddwyn visible at the mouth of the Menai Straits.

Further north, to Eryri, the muscular mountain range leads the eye east, inland to the escarpments and plains of Blaenau, before coming south again, where, beyond Pencaenewydd, Glasfrynfawr is easily located by the lake. He can make out the shapes of horses and cattle, indistinct figures, and imagines he can see Jane with the baby on her hip, though in reality it could be any one of his workers.

As Wiliam descends the ages peel away, past the banked walls, sisters of hawthorn and curious sheep, gorse flowers and roused crows. In the field above Pencaenewydd he lies flat on his back, his skin the same colour as the bleached grass. This spot is equidistant between Bryn Rhydd, his childhood home, and his own place. At one hundred and eighty acres, Glasfryn is bigger than his dad's farm ever was.

Like his father Rhisiart before him, although Wiliam makes all the decisions about the farm, he does not own it – will never own it. A tenant farmer, he has a certain independence, he tells himself.

The warden of Llanarmon church, Rhisiart was a devout Christian. Wiliam remembers his father's joy when his brother John – the oldest son – went up to Oxford to study Divinity. Rhisiart was so proud. It cost a fortune, but the church helped, the old parson Evan being a friend of his dad's.

Unlike his dad or his brother, Wiliam has never had the slightest interest in religion. He goes to church, of course, but that is just habitual – everybody does. When he thinks about his brother now, he remembers John's humour, intellect and charisma.

His mind shies away from the pictures of his old dad,

bereft and broken-hearted, watching helplessly as John spiralled out of control.

William rouses himself and carries on across the field towards Glasfryn. Nettles sting, horseflies rise up to greet him – he swats them away with both hands but they follow him, hovering around his head. In the hedgerow brambles snag and catch, not wanting to let him go. He moves, from the furnace to the grove, and the entrance to Glasfrynfawr.

The way is dark with undergrowth – cow parsley, elderflower and foxgloves so tall as to form an arch overhead, bracken, hawthorn and blackthorn forming the backbone. The air is thick with the scent of meadowsweet, almost sickly.

The track is almost unrecognisable from its winter self, the holes filled with ash, the packed earth a pale cream which shines in the light. The walls of his house are traced with a pale lichen, the blooms of greys and greens spawn, the rough heads set close to the stone. Inside it is cool, the blaze of the sun does not penetrate.

Glasfrynfawr

August 1738

Glasfryn is a handsome building facing south, exposed to the sea wind on all four sides. This parish of Pencaenewydd, Llangybi and Llanarmon is where Wiliam's father Rhisart grew up, his grandfather Morus and his forefathers. Wiliam is living in the same place his ancestors lived – it is the place he comes from.

The farmhouse is the heart of an industrious community, with a smithy, dairy, laundry, stables and cowshed all positioned around a central well.

Wiliam brings the busyness of the outside world in with him. He comes up to change, to check how Jane is.

He pulls off his shirt and buttons on a clean one, standing with his back to the window and leans over the bed to kiss her. The shape of his face familiar, eyes smiling, warm stubble against her cheek. He rises to go back down to the kitchen, to find something to eat.

'Are you selling kisses?' she asks, tucked straight under the blanket, hair spread out around her, unwilling to let him go.

'Why yes,' he says, letting the door fall from his hand and turning back.

'How much are they?' she murmurs, his warm lips against hers.

'Very, very expensive,' he says, kissing her softly in between each slow, mock-serious word.

She laughs low with delight, feels his hand cool against her.

'But not cash up front?' she chides, hoping.

The shirt comes off again and she watches him, how the light catches the contours of his body, the curve of his spine.

She can hear the dog barking through the open window. The wasps buzz louder and quieter, neither inside nor out. He comes in with her then, lies against her and she rises above him, covering them with her long hair. His body warm and firm, her lips like rosebuds, hips like apple blossom, all for him. She comes quickly, as easily as breathing, fluid, wet, jagged breathing, next to him. They lie side by side in the big bed, becoming conscious of the sounds of the world outside. Her eyes flicker open to see his looking at her – there is the question in them.

Downstairs, the heat of the bedroom dissolves into a conversation about practicalities, as she moves around the kitchen.

'These damned wasps.' She clears more from the windowsill by the sink. She folds the cloth, catches the wasps, opens the window and puts them outside. Every day wasps, thin, torpid, unable to understand the flat window pane, battling against it incessantly.

'Do you think there is a nest?'

What she means is that she wants him to find the nest and kill the wasps.

'They'll be gone soon enough,' he says, reaching for the bread.

'Soon it will be too cold for them to survive.'

And the kettle boils and the baby wakes and he puts his boots back on.

Later Jane picks blackberries, full and ripe, the best of them falling into the basket at her touch. She can't bear to pass them without stopping and eats them on the roadside, hands stained purple.

In the evening Wiliam sets out for Llangybi. The

swallows fly low over the fields, circulating between the legs of cattle that graze uninterrupted. The drizzle falls as a light mist, and caught in the grass seed-heads, the pink bleeds into gold. After the taut heat you can feel the earth relax and give way to this slow saturation.

Above Pencaenewydd he sees Bryn Rhydd in the distance, the straight avenue leading to his childhood home where he played with his brother and sisters.

It was a big deal, John going up to Oxford. When Wiliam visited him there he found his brother changed somehow, affected perhaps by the rarefied environment he found himself in.

Over the week of his visit he realised that the tall tales his brother told were actually only slightly different versions of the same story – fantastical, egotistical stories, founded on ideas of grandeur and persecution. His delusions were presented as actualities, whereas they could not possibly be so – to be presented as such was embarrassing. Wiliam did not know what to do, shocked when his brother offered him whisky at eight in the morning.

John had lost the capacity to make rational connections and instead formed new, entirely fictitious ones. Paranoid and delusional, it became difficult to make sense of him. John could not be found where he said he was going to be, but was instead holed up somewhere on a three-day bender.

When Wiliam tried to talk to him about it, John avoided him, or placated his brother with long, sad reflections on his own failings. Others were calmed and charmed in this way, but not Wiliam, though his concern made absolutely no difference to John's behaviour.

Eventually, tired and exasperated, John's friends began to distance themselves, and as they did the shield of their friendship dropped, leaving him exposed to the disasters waiting to happen. One day it was as though suddenly the veil was lifted and he had shifted, from a funny drunk to a pariah. The accidents he had so narrowly missed up until that point began to happen in painful real time. His debts were called in.

'It's a waste of his time and his talent'

Wiliam remembers keenly his dad's despair, having to bail out his oldest son, yet again.

'He's no use to himself nor anyone else'

Even now, walking through the woods, Wiliam can feel the vestiges of an old shame rising in him, a red flush that spreads across his chest and up his neck, that has nothing to do with the energy of walking.

Towards the end his brother smelt strange – a fermented odour that stuck to his teeth and seeped out of his pores. John was yellow and grey, as weathered as a man in old age, rather than one in his mid-twenties. He found it difficult to talk or stand upright for more than a few minutes and would sink to his knees, short of breath.

Wiliam arrives at the pub in Llangybi. Later that night he will bounce off the windows, ricochet between doorways, fuelled by whisky and who knows what. He is shouting, but does not know it.

Pencaenewydd
1738

In September the morning fog comes thick against the window. Fine webs hang in the gorse, forming pockets of white moisture within their fragile hold. Eventually rain falls as air is forced to rise over the mountains. It fills the leaves with its sound, relentlessly, remorselessly drowning the track in deep brown puddles.

The brambles sag with defeat and all green gives up its colour. Yellowing, browning, a slimy mosaic of fallen leaves disintegrates on the path.

It can rain like this all day, silent, thin, vertical. When it stops the fog moves in to sit like a vapour blanket around the house. You can't see past the ash tree, the air is so thick with this palest grey.

Knee-deep in November, Wiliam sees himself as one from afar as they bury his mum in Llanarmon. They line up on the pew, Jane holding the baby, Mary, Margaret and Elin holding hands. Huw, the oldest, pale and serious in his dark suit.

Wiliam turns to whisper to his son, so that his face is in profile, eyes set within creased laughter lines. His coat is misted with rain, the hair which falls to his collar similarly matted and damp. He is slightly unkempt, because of the elements, the feeling and energy of life in the fields is contained in that.

The vicar is the same man who buried his father, *Richardus* carved deep into the stone. Now his mum lies alongside his dad. Wiliam's first wife Mary is buried here, his brother John too. Now his mum's passing seems like the end of an old world, of signs and relics.

Wiliam is the last to leave the graveside, behind Jane in her cape, best shoes and hat. They walk up the path of muted tones, the bare branches of the tree whisked in the wind so that everything – the figures and the landscape – become almost merged into one.

That month Wiliam goes to Sunday service. Like the rest of them, he is bored stiff by vicar Nanney's sermons, but attendance at church is a legal obligation. He thinks that the clergy themselves are tired of it too, only coming out occasionally to deliver their platitudes, their voices falling like silver on cut straw. Vicar Nanney – like most of the clergy – doesn't speak Welsh, so the entire service is in English. As most of the congregation – Wiliam's friends and neighbours – don't understand much English, the meaning of the sermon is entirely lost on them.

Listening to Nanney's sanctimonious drone this Sunday, Wiliam thinks about the vicar's predecessor, the old parson Evan Griffiths. The reason he can even afford to farm a place as big as Glasfryn is largely due to Evan.

Whilst John was up at Oxford Evan stayed with Rhisiart's family. He taught Wiliam some English and Latin, as Rhisiart swore not to invest any money on his second son's education, given his experience with his first son. When the parson died, he left most of his estate to Rhisiart, and when his dad died Wiliam inherited the lot – a substantial amount, enough to establish him at Glasfrynfawr.

After the service Wiliam joins his mates in the pub opposite the church, so close you barely have to draw breath before leaving the one and arriving at the other. He spends a vital few hours here, the customary 'just the one' multiplying exponentially. When they eventually pour out, the short afternoon has merged into dark night. Reverberating with camaraderie, he weaves his way into the valley and begins the regular walk home along the riverbank.

Dogs bark on the other side of the water, which rushes by unseen. At the beech tree there is the fork in the track, and he begins the climb up Garn Bentyrch, struggling to find his footing in the mud, cursing the moonless night. He stops at what should be the stone outcrop and squints into the darkness around him.

Straining to see into the distance, he eventually spots a light that must be Glasfryn, about a mile away. He sets out towards it, stumbling over the rough ground, but when he comes closer sees that the light is not Glasfryn at all, but his neighbour Francis' farm, Caertyddyn. There is a light in the downstairs window and he can see bowed heads and hear Francis reading aloud to his family.

Wiliam stands at the gate and listens for a minute, takes a piss, takes his bearings and sets out towards home.

As Caertyddyn's light fades he realises that he has lost his bearings somehow, and has not the slightest idea where he is. He staggers this way and that and is tempted to lie down under the gorse, but then catches the glimmer of Glasfryn's light in the distance and sets out towards it.

The closer he gets to the light the more his heart sinks, as it becomes apparent that the house he is walking towards is not Glasfryn at all, but Caertyddyn, meaning he has just walked around in a big circle.

Wiliam flushes deep with embarrassment, as though there was anyone there to see him – there is no-one, only the light from the downstairs window and Francis' voice, reading aloud.

Wiliam's confidence, like the alcohol, has evaporated. Now entirely sober he turns carefully towards home. It's a mile to the west – it's easy, he tells himself – he has done it a thousand times.

He walks purposefully for a while, concentrating hard until he knows for sure that he has lost his way again. It is near midnight and he does not know in the slightest which way he is facing, or what path he has taken. He is simultaneously hot and cold.

The third time he sees the light he thinks that it has to be Glasfryn, but when he gets closer once again he knows he has found himself at Caertyddyn.

The night is dead black, apart from the patch of light from the farmhouse window cast on the ground.

'Gwyliwch gan hynny; am na wyddoch na'r dydd na'r awr y daw Mab y dyn.'

'Watch therefore, for ye know neither the day nor the hour wherein the Son of man cometh.'

Wiliam finally listens, seeing but unseen as old man Francis finishes the parable and lays the book to one side. He then kneels, holds his palms pressed together and begins a prayer which encompasses the whole world.

Francis prays for forgiveness, for himself and his family, his unknowing friends and neighbours, and finally

Wiliam hears the old man praying for *him*.

In the farmyard, Wiliam feels a sheet of white light enter the crown of his head and flow into his body, down his neck, across his shoulders, into his chest and lungs. It flows through every organ – muscles, nerves and bones, deep into his being. Down the length of his arms, he feels old energy released through the palms of his hands, through the tips of his fingers, into the night air and in its place comes this new limitless white light.

In an instant he understands himself to be as one with all things, a part of the whole cosmos. The light permeates his whole body, into his stomach, down his legs into his feet planted firmly on the ground. The light is steady and brilliant, like the sun's glare on still water.

Old man Francis, having finished his prayers, takes the light and heads up the stairs. Wiliam turns silently for home, finding his way this time as easily as though it were daylight.

Capel

1739

At dawn the tree is a visual shock, a meditative hit of gold and green, flaring upright and outward to the flaming tips.

He rises before everyone else and still can't catch it, can't capture it – the flush, the roar, the incandescent light of early morning as his soul exults. A crow sits there, black and shiny. Full, damp, observing – every bird knows what is to come.

Francis' words have become imprinted on Wiliam's mind, working on him in a profound way.

Wiliam begins to meditate in the very early morning and late at night, in the cowshed out back of the kitchen. He makes sure that this time doesn't affect the family or working life – everything he needs to do on the farm still gets done – in fact his focus becomes sharper, his concentration enhanced.

Over the next few weeks and months his family and workers all notice the difference, but cannot put their finger on the change. He is more aware somehow, more considerate than he used to be.

Wiliam's new routine establishes itself into a pattern where he rises at four, leaving the bed silently. Jane slides over to fill the empty space, their movements shifting and realigning to accommodate this new element.

He goes out of the back of the house to the small byre where they store oats and hay, and kneels on a mat he has brought for this purpose. This meditation is a constant discipline, a private routine, his voice a surprise in the first glimmers of day.

He prays for his family, then extends this prayer outwards, to encompass his neighbours and all of humanity. Working in the fields, at every hour of the day wherever he may be, he prays internally, reverently, so that everything becomes imbued with a powerful light, originating in his solar plexus and radiating out.

After lunch Wiliam slips out of the kitchen and makes his way across the yard to the byre. One of the young labourers, Morris, often notices his boss disappearing quietly after the meal, as the rest of the farmhands chat in the aftermath.

He wonders where Wiliam goes and one day follows him secretly, watching Wiliam cross the yard to the little shed and disappear inside.

Peering through the side of the door Morris spies Wiliam kneeling on the mat, his forehead flat on the slate floor. He is quite taken aback, embarrassed to be witnessing this, yet too fascinated to leave.

Morris watches for a while, before slipping back into the house. He doesn't say anything to anyone, but the next time he sees Wiliam going out, he follows him again, listening to the prayers that Wiliam is intoning, unaware of the young man's presence.

After a few times of this Morris confesses to Wiliam that he has been following him, and the two men begin to sit in the barn together.

Over the next few months, another of the labourers joins Wiliam and Morris in the barn. Now there are three of the Glasfryn household exhibiting a certain sort of difference. The way they hold themselves, the way they speak, is more considered, more serious somehow.

People begin to look at them sideways, particularly Wiliam, who has not been to the pub once in the past couple of months.

Occasionally it drives Jane mad, her husband's new-found piety. He is careful and deliberate, with a self-awareness that drives her to distraction. She wishes he would take to the whisky again, to come back warm and rounded.

Sometimes she feels that her every move is subject to scrutiny. People may study the Bible, but they don't actually *abide* by it, she thinks, whereas Wiliam follows the words absolutely, his adoration of Christ making him seem vulnerable and naive. It embarrasses and irritates her – why can't he be like other people – like he used to be? Why does he have to take it so *seriously*?

People have started talking, particularly because he never goes to the pub anymore, like he used to. She remembers how easy it used to be, and feels now as though a layer of comfort and oblivion has been stripped away.

Wiliam seems so absolute, whereas she feels more flexible, readily accepting the inequalities in life. His wife loves him enough to know that he is discovering something essential. Jane can tell where he is up to by the set of his mouth, the cast of his eyes.

She does not find it easy, particularly when there is a flare-up of pious opinion – then she finds it humourless, stifling and restrictive. She gets on with her own things, not letting his moods affect her too much, knowing there is an internal dialogue within him, a battle to equate the ideals of perfection with the imperfections of the everyday.

The holy flare-ups pass, like a high fever, and gradually things settle to a peaceful equilibrium, where he is more ordinary again, and they rub along more or less like they used to, but it is always there, she knows, this deep analysis of himself and others.

Wiliam feels a clarity he has not known before and with it a commitment to challenge the inequalities surrounding him. He attends church regularly, becoming increasingly dissatisfied with the vicar's interpretations of the sermons and the general lassitude of the church as a whole.

The vicar, Edward Nanney, has accepted a posting in Wales, seeing it as a stepping stone to a better job elsewhere – that is, back in England. There is nothing unusual in that – Wales is generally viewed by the establishment as an ignorant country, its people immoral. Vicar Nanney – like many of his peers – does not speak Welsh, so the services are in English only.

Unlike many of his neighbours, William is bilingual and literate, able to speak and write in English. Most of the community are Welsh only and many of them, though speaking their language, are not literate – they can't read nor write in their mother tongue. There is little to no chance of their learning either, as there are no schools to teach them.

The Bible in the church pulpit is written in both English and Welsh, but as most of the congregation can't read; they simply listen to the vicar's English sermon, which they barely understand. It seems to Wiliam that there exists a world of difference between the church and ordinary people. If most people can't read the Bible, nor hear it in their own language, it is difficult to find relevance – a meaningful connection – between the Christian message and everyday life.

It is rare enough that there is any church service at all, the clergy more often than not tucked up in their comfortable houses, wallowing in a kind of spiritual torpor which has spread across the land. Church ministers offer no moral guidance and are seemingly entirely indifferent to the idea of the spriritual enlightenment of their parishioners, or any idea of change at all.

The only other religious service in the area is the small independent congregation at Capel Helyg. Francis Caertyddyn tells Wiliam that a minister from south Wales – Lewis Rees – is visiting and invites his neighbour to the service. As Wiliam enters the chapel he is struck by the lack of embellishments – no shining platters, no gold and silver, no windows of coloured glass. It is as though things have been stripped back to their essence.

The congregation look after their chapel collectively, independent of outside rule – there is no bishop or chancellor and altogether less hierarchy than within the church.

Wiliam sits next to Francis and looks around at the congregation, many of whom nod their acknowledgement of him. Wiliam knows this congregation suffer a lot of persecution being worshippers in an independent church. 'Nonconformists' or 'Dissenters' are Protestants who do not conform to the established church, they disagree with the state being involved in religious matters. As such these nonconformists encounter a range of social disadvantages – they are forbidden to hold public office, work in schools, the civil service or go to university. These are the laws of the land, established and upheld in an attempt to quash dissent.

Although the Nonconformists are legally allowed to hold an independent service at Capel Helyg, their attendance at the Anglican church is compulsory. Everyone has to attend church services and anyone not attending pays a hefty fine. So in order to meet the intricate legal requirements of the state, Nonconformists do both – communion at church to satisfy the state and worship at a chapel, independent of Anglican rule.

The minister Lewis Rees has taken to the platform, in front of a packed house.

'Mae'r golau'r nefoedd yn cychwyn gwawrio!'

Immediately Wiliam notices the fundamental difference between church and chapel, in that this service is in Cymraeg, the language of the people.

Lewis Rees speaks directly to the congregation, as one of them. He is insightful, powerful, resonant – everything, in fact, that Vicar Nanney is not. He brings them news of the independent movement in south and mid Wales.

'The dawn of heaven is starting to break! There is a great uprising in the south, where a minister called Howel Harris is going around the villages, preaching in the fields, like some great plough, turning up the land.'

The minister's words express a profound Christian attitude and awake in Wiliam a deeper conviction. At the end of the service the congregation gather around the minister and talk animatedly to one another, refreshed, animated, as though they have woken from a deep sleep.

Word spreads, and over the next few weeks the numbers attending Capel Helyg increase, attracted by the new Nonconformist minister. Wiliam starts to attend both church and chapel. Often after the chapel services he stays behind and discusses the state of the country with Francis Caertyddyn, Lewis Rees and the others.

Rees describes to them in great detail what is happening in the south. Under the auspices of the Anglican minister, Griffith Jones, Howel Harris is making his way up through mid-Wales, changing the landscape as he goes – establishing free schools in rural towns, teaching ordinary people to read and write.

'Is it possible to get him to come up here, do you think, this Howel Harris?' asks Wiliam.

'He might,' muses Lewis. 'There is already one of

Griffith Jones' men up here in the north, in Y Bala.'

The congregation discuss it amongst themselves and it is agreed that Lewis will ask Howel Harris to visit Llangybi with the idea of setting up a free school there.

Wiliam walks home quite buoyant and intent, with some other feeling he can't quite identify. It takes him the three miles back to Glasfryn before he has worked out that the feeling is excitement, a smile inside.

Griffith

Short and unprepossessing, Griffith Jones begins his sermons quite conversationally, building to a fervour that has his listeners transfixed. The large congregation in his small church are faithful, but Griffith has come to realise that they are not really able to understand the messages within the scriptures.

They can't read and are too afraid to ask for help, so Griffith has begun to set them the task of remembering passages from the Bible by rote. They then read these sections from the big book together the next week, tracing out the lines, beginning to recognise the pattern of letters, words and eventually whole sentences.

Griffith takes it slowly and gently, so that no-one feels intimidated. People open up more readily this way, and he is able to explain the passages they have remembered, week on week, month after month. He uses Bishop Morgan's Bible, a beautiful translation articulating a depth of Cymraeg not found in normal, everyday speech.

It is wonderful to him to see the transformation take place as his congregation gradually become readers. Those once hesitant men and women become confident, articulate: empowered. His fellow clergy are outraged at the very idea of ordinary working men and women being taught to read and write, complaining to the Bishop that they cannot see the sense in it.

Griffith's reputation goes before him. The numbers in his congregation continue to increase and criticism of his methods begins to escalate, as the churchmen feel their superiority being challenged by this unconventional minister's approach.

Sometimes the clergy lock Griffith out of the church, forcing him to hold the services in the graveyard and in the fields beyond. Thousands of people gather to hear him, raising the level of establishment outrage even further. Griffith is summoned to the Bishop and prosecuted for ignoring Church conventions. But they cannot dismiss him, so Griffith perseveres, continuing to hold his services weekdays and Sundays, regardless.

As well as having his enemies, Griffith has wealthy, influential supporters, who back him in his radical ambitions to set up an educational institution – a school – free to all – which will convert people from a life trapped in ignorance to one of literacy and freedom.

The institution is funded by these aristocratic and philanthropic supporters and Griffith's ideas of a 'circulating school' are realised. The teachers – ordained ministers – are sent to a needy town or village. Using the Bible as their curriculum, they teach the locals to read and write in Cymraeg, their first language. After a couple of months in each place the teachers move on to the next place, apply the same method, then move onto the next town, before returning to the first destination and beginning the cycle again – hence the term 'circulating'. Those pupils that have learnt to read and write pass on that skill to others – so that literacy spreads like wildfire.

Griffith employs more and more teachers, interviewing them meticulously, his aim to find truly religious men, whose faith is underpinned by a love of all mankind. He chooses Nonconformist ministers because they, unlike their Church of England counterparts, have an altogether more sober and religious approach.

Some of them, like Daniel Rowland and Howel Harris, are extraordinary orators. He appoints Harris as the superintendent, whose job it is to check on all the schools across the different counties, starting in the south and making his way through mid-Wales up to the north.

The Anglican church does not like it one bit, feeling the threat to its authority, its supremacy, its very core. The clergy draw together in opposition to this emerging wave of 'new religionists'. They raise the level of complaint to the Bishop and begin to take matters into their own hands, in a bid to keep the schools out of their parishes. In their sermons vicars actively encourage their flock to form gangs of opposition against these visiting school teachers, these heinous Nonconformists with their irreligious new ways. Churchmen and women, curates and sextons, normal Christian parishioners, form organised gangs, incited by the sermons from the Anglican pulpit.

Harris

Howel Harris rides up hills and across fields, propelled by an inner force, fuelled by an indomitable love, charged with the splendour of the Mighty.

He preaches to labourers, farmhands and housewives – most of these people who gather to hear him have never read the Bible, but find great meaning in his words.

Harris knows there is a point in his sermon where he becomes simply a vessel, a conduit for a higher message. He can hear himself speaking, but the words are formed outside of himself somehow. The message streams out of him with profound lucidity – he cannot predict when it will happen, but he knows when it does, and the audience know it too.

The hymns give them a form of expression, a way

of articulating their fears, sadness and hopes. When they sing, a thousand voices discover harmonies and resonances which blast apart old uncertainties, lifting their spirits high. It's a powerful combination of forces, compelling and infectious.

At the peak of this ecstasy, it is his steady words that bring them safely back down. Later, alone in the hostel, he is empty – a husk. Even in this exhausted state, Harris holds onto this attachment, forever seeking the ultimate union. He writes until dawn, questioning his faith, and at the same time feeling his mission to be so wonderful that it is imperative. The intensity wears him out.

He cannot avoid it, has committed his life to it, this expression of the deepest truth. It changes people's lives – he has witnessed over and over again, the moment they discard their past selves and step into enlightenment. Hearing him, men's perception of life is transformed.

Harris goes places the church just doesn't go – preaching in the fields, streets and poorhouses, reaching out to people in a language they understand. From this sermon in Pembrokeshire he will make the long journey north, stopping at towns and villages along the way, inspecting the existing schools and giving authority for new ones. He averages about forty miles a day – by the time he reaches Y Bala he has covered around one hundred and fifty miles.

He has been warned about the reception that might

await him in Y Bala, and sure enough, on the long road into town he finds a rabble in the middle of the road, barring the way ahead. The vicar stands in the centre, holding up one outstretched hand – the other grasps a wooden club.

'You can stop there!' the vicar shouts.

Harris keeps the horse moving.

'I have no intention of deliberately offending anyone' Harris says levelly, moving through the crowd, their curses flung against his receding back, leaving them impotent and outraged.

On entering the town centre he is met by the young schoolmaster Jenkin Morgan, who welcomes him and shows him where he will be staying. A large crowd have gathered, drawn by the preacher's reputation. Jenkin leads him inside the hostel, explaining to Harris that the church have been working on the locals, fuelling them with liquor in preparation for this visit.

Harris is keen to stay in the street and talk openly to everybody, but Jenkin entreats him to give the sermon inside, where they are surrounded by friends, out of harm's way.

Harris wastes no time. His audience are locals, mostly farmers, independent worshippers and their families. All of them strive to ignore the increasing racket outside. They can see the feet of people scaling the walls of the house, like monkeys, shouting, rattling the windows, battering the doors.

Harris raises his voice.

'Vanity of vanities. All is vanity. What profit has a man from all his labour in which he works under the sun? One generation passes away, and another generation comes, but the earth abides for ever.'

Harris expounds on what he has just read, telling them about their souls, about the love of God, denouncing the gentry and the clergy in the process. Outside the women scream profanities, the men are hammering the windows and the doors are beginning to splinter.

'We have to get you out of here,' Jenkin bundles Harris out of the door, where someone in the crowd grabs him by the collar, lifts him up and headbutts him square on the nose. As Harris sinks to the ground, he is covered in kicks and blows.

The women stone him and smear him with human excrement. Eventually, either out of pity or fear of having killed him, they leave off and Harris is able to drag himself the short distance to his hostel, a trail of blood in his wake.

The next day he rides from Y Bala through Trawsfynydd and across Traeth Mawr, arriving at Wiliam's house Glasfrynfawr on the Saturday evening. Over dinner with his hosts, Harris recounts the events of the night before.

'It's strange,' he says, 'but as I sank to the ground, I felt all my fears vanish. Even as I knew my life was in danger, I felt as though I were established on a great rock.'

Wiliam looks at Harris slightly askance, realising that the man's convictions will drive him to preach whatever the cost. It evokes in Wiliam both a feeling of admiration and a certain wariness.

'You were lucky to escape with your life,' Wiliam says. 'You are very courageous.'

Harris shakes his head. 'Not at all. I am by nature timid – what courage I have is a gift from God. I meet him in all things, and the strength of the love he shows me enables me to go through all oppositions.'

That evening Harris discusses with Wiliam the Methodist movement, the Wesley brothers and their Oxford society, specifically set up to promote spiritual development.

'Why is the church so set against them?' Wiliam asks. 'I can't understand it, when we are all essentially after the same thing, surely?'

'The church feels threatened,' Harris says. 'The Methodists take food into poorhouses and jails, talking to people the Anglican clergy aren't remotely interested in. They reach people in ways that the existing church cannot – it is an embarrassment to the church.

Thousands of people have been enlightened by John

Wesley and his kind – thousands!'.

'But the wrath of the church is so set against them,' says Wiliam. 'They are under attack in real and physical ways, like you yourself are.'

Harris nods. 'Yes, that's true, but far more people are with us than against us.' He sits back in his chair and opens his palms out wide.

'The people who attack us – the Anglican church and their lot – are in a minority. Even their violence means that we are taking the Word into the right places. We're not shut up behind doors in some elitist institution but taking the word of truth out to the people, effecting real change'.

They talk late into the night, discussing the church's antipathy to independence and the idea of a free school at Llangybi. Harris supports it, and suggests that Jenkin Morgan would be a good man for the job, being able to travel there after his stint in Llanuwchllyn, near Y Bala.

On Sunday they rise early.

'Is there is a service we can go to this morning?' Harris asks.

'Certainly,' says Wiliam. 'There is a new vicar taking the service at Llannor church. His name's John Owen – I haven't heard him before, but word is that he is an eloquent speaker.'

After breakfast they head out for Llannor and by the

time they arrive the church is almost full, the two men managing to squeeze onto a pew at the back. Listening to the vicar take the reading, Wiliam thinks Owen's reputation to be perfectly justified. The hymns are sung in good voice before Owen takes to the pulpit to deliver his sermon. The silence deepens in the dramatic pause just before Owen speaks. He looks down at the book in front of him portentously, then lifts his head and glares across the parishioners.

'These *Dissenters*,' he hisses.

Wiliam sits bolt upright.

'Independents, *Nonconformists*, Methodists – call them what you will, they need to be *driven out* from our land.' Vicar Owen slices the air directly above the parishioners heads.

Wiliam looks at Harris, who does not meet his eyes, but stares straight ahead. The congregation gaze up at their shepherd, the vicar John Owen.

'*Dissenters*. There is one of them on his way *here, now* – a heretic coming to our county, as I speak!'

Owen's voice rises in outrage, he bangs the wooden pulpit with his fist and the congregation, alarmed, begin to consult one another. The vicar grips his hands on each side of the pulpit, his arms straight, his knuckles white. Then he points at his congregation, moving his finger across one and all.

'He may *look* like you or I, but be warned, he is Minister to the Devil!'

The crowd gasp and Owen continues ominously.

'His name is *Howel Harris*. Be warned, good people, and *be in no doubt* – he is the epitome of all that is evil.'

The noise level rises, each parishioner urgently conferring with his neighbour. Wiliam and Harris sit like statues. Eventually the vicar raises his hand and the crowd fall silent.

'It is a duty incumbent upon you, out of love for church and country, to join against this man. This Harris is a poison that will destroy your estates and your immortal souls!'

Mightily roused, the congregation launch into the final hymn, before filing out into the churchyard. All the talk is about this new danger, this devil of a man heading their way. Wiliam inches out, silent amidst his boisterous neighbours, desperate to be out of there but frustrated by the agonisingly slow pace of the people before him.

'Wiliam Prichard!' an old friend approaches him, claps him on the shoulder.

'What did you make of it?'

Wiliam doesn't answer – perhaps he didn't hear.

'Wiliam Prisiart, how did you like the sermon?'

'I didn't.' Wiliam looks grim, ashen.

'What do you mean?' his friend asks, taken aback.

'I didn't like it one bit.'

'How's that?'

'The things he says are not true.' Wiliam is trapped in the slow-moving crowd, one eye fixed on Harris, who has moved ahead of him, closer to the vicar at the gate. As Wiliam responds to his friend he realises exactly what is going to unfold. He sees Harris introduce himself to vicar Owen, the vicar's realisation and recoil. Wiliam pushes hastily through the crowd and reaches Harris, pulling him away through the gate as the word spreads through the congregation as to who exactly is in their midst. They reach the horses and ride away, pelted by stones the crowd have picked up from the church path.

Safely home at Glasfryn Wiliam describes what happened to Jane, and she can see how shaken her husband is.

'I can't believe what I just heard – this blatant incitement to violence' says Wiliam.

'Yes,' Harris says, gazing out of the window. 'But the people want to hear it – they are looking for an enemy, anyone other than themselves to blame.'

Wiliam is getting used to his guest's prophetic way with words. He thinks his own voice sounds reedy in comparison.

'It staggers me, the reserves of control you must have, to resist this terrible aggression,'

Harris looks straight at him.

'It's not easy,' he says. 'It is hard to come out of ourselves and believe in Christ.

To despair in ourselves and to trust in another is a work above all nature. I find myself often so chained up that I have no more light, love, life, desire for God than a stone, but am hard, dry, dead, dull, drowsy, and so would remain for ever were it not for the free grace that comes and takes me up.'

Harris leaves early the next day, riding along the coast to Penmorfa in a limpid morning, the clouds' curves and billows echoed by the Rhinogydd, the watery blues and browns riven with a strip of luminous sunlight on the surface of the sea. As he waits for the ferry, his fellow travellers glare at him with murderous intent.

Kitchen School

1740

Having been successful in getting Harris' approval for the school, the Capel Helyg congregation are keen to move things along. The first thing they need to do is find somewhere to hold the classes.

'If you could get some responsible man in your neighbourhood – a churchgoer – it may be worth him approaching the church to see if you could hold the school there,' Lewis Rees says.

They decide that Wiliam, with his lifelong connection to the church, is perfect for the job, and ask him to make the request of the new parish vicar, John Owen.

Wiliam is hesitant at first, having witnessed at first hand the vicar's strong opposition to anything to do with the Independent movement. But he reasons that his family's close relationship with the church – they helped put John through College, after all – and the worthy nature of the request, will supercede any misgivings the vicar may have.

He meets vicar Owen in the church house and explains the idea, the origins of the initiative and its success to date.

'The Circulating Schools come under the auspices of the Anglican church, so everything will be carried out properly. It will be free, open to all, and will not cost the church a penny' says Wiliam, going on to explain that one of Griffith Jones' men, the experienced schoolteacher Jenkin Morgan, will hold the classes.

'We would be grateful for your permission to hold the school in the church house' Wiliam concludes.

'You will do no such thing.' Vicar John Owen is set stolid behind his desk.

Wiliam leans forward, not sure if the vicar has understood the nature and breadth of the proposal.

'Vicar, this school will benefit the whole community. It will lift men, women and children alike out of a life of illiteracy.'

John Owen is having none of it.

'These teachers are Methodists and *Dissenters* – troublemakers, the lot of them. We will not have their sort here.'

Owen continues in this tone, and eventually, seeing there is no way to convince him, Wiliam leans back.

'Well, if you have authority over your church, I have authority over my own kitchen,' he says quietly. 'He can keep the school there.'

He bids the Vicar a polite farewell and rides home to Glasfryn, where he clears out the old barn and lights a fire in the hearth.

'We're holding the school here' he tells Jane.

The barn is separate to the main house, it will need some rearranging, but it can be done. The schoolteacher will sleep above the classroom.

Meanwhile Francis Caertyddyn sets off for Y Bala, forty miles to the east, over the wide sands of Penmorfa, up across the moorland of Trawsfynydd, to find Jenkin Morgan. He is successful in securing the young teacher and they return together to Llangybi, riding past Francis' own home direct to Glasfrynfawr, so that nobody can gossip about a Church of England schoolmaster living with a Nonconformist.

So the kitchen school is established at Glasfrynfawr. Jenkin teaches a mixture of pupils, mostly youngsters during the day and adults in the evening, when the farm work is done. They begin to form a new routine at Glas-frynfawr and word of the classes spreads.

As the school's popularity grows, Vicar John Owen

uses his substantial authority to cultivate fear and mistrust about it. Rumours begin to circulate that the school is *unclean*, morally and spiritually, that Wiliam and Jenkin Morgan are *adulterers*.

Over time the rumours become wilder – that Wiliam and Morgan are traders, waiting for a ship to come in to a nearby cove to spirit the children away, that they are agitators, forming a conspiracy against the King.

An old friend who 'thinks he should know' tells Wiliam about this, who experiences a range of emotions in the telling. There is initial shock – he was not expecting it. He feels a betrayal of trust, that the church should treat him this way after his family's long faithfulness. The next emotion is quiet recognition – *of course* he knew it would come to this. Instinctively he had always held a part of himself back from the church, after all, and now he understands why.

The friend who tells him is himself taken aback by the malicious rumours that are being spread by the vicar.

'He is dangerous,' he says to Wiliam. 'Keep away from him.'

Wiliam continues to observe the emotions passing through him so quickly – anger, upset, followed by a cold, calm withdrawal. He battles with himself for several days, struggling with the concept of forgiveness, wondering about defence and about the correct way forward. He understands that something significant has happened, that a delicate balance has been tipped.

His neighbours are vitriolic. The more they lash him with their tongues, the easier it becomes, until condemning Wiliam becomes second nature to them, a common ground where they can unleash all their anger. They do not trouble themselves with alternative perspectives, with nuances or subtleties which may point to a different version of their story. Wiliam has been introduced as a threat, and now the die has been cast. He is not one of them – he is different, and that is enough.

This venomous opinion lives as an invisible thing, never to be captured or held up to the light of day to be examined. It slips from person to person, growing within them as a dark mould over their souls, revealed only when they are with like-minded people. It is an unimaginable rot, when faced with their superficial pleasantries and bright smiles.

The vicious words leave the gossipers wanting more. When one layer of lies is firmly established, so as to become fact, another layer can be formed on top of it. Thick and thin layers are applied in this way, each one created from a bit of gossip here, a damning aspersion there, a dusting of grave opinion, a sprinkling of doubt, a handful of outrage.

It's a group endeavour, the layers shifting and altering

to the vagaries of their creators, until, finding the right colour, just the right pitch, they fix to form a thick veneer – a
hard, impenetrable shell. Wiliam becomes a construct of
their avidly-tended hate and this becomes their favourite
subject.

Having spent so much time and energy in the forming
of their subject – that is Wiliam – the players can now
watch the game unfold. Whatever Wiliam says or does,
it will always be within the construct they have made for
him. So even if Wiliam does only good every day of his
life, from here to eternity, he will never be able to pierce
the hard shell that encloses him in the eyes of his detrac-
tors – never be able to change their opinion through word
or deed, or so he feels.

Some of Wiliam's neighbours feel uncomfortable
occasionally about the way they have portrayed him, their
consciences rearing after a particularly spiteful bout of
gossip. Every aspect of his life is commented on – what
he says, how he says it. Multiple meanings can be formed
to suit the group narrative, as instigated by the church,
that Wiliam and his Nonconformist brethren are dangerous heretics.

Not all of Wiliam's neighbours buy into this, however, some of them managing to steer a middle ground,
quietly registering events and remaining impartial.

It is not always clear what drives the motives of his

enemies – the nature of the exercise is that it lives in the dark – but anger, fear, jealousy and intolerance all have their place. They don't look deeply into their own motives but feel great justification and irrefutable rightness in their own moral certitude.

Anger, jealousy, hurt – sometimes it is just good sport. Sometimes it is just tapping into that curious human tendency that in undermining someone else some people feel better about themselves and their circumstances.

It is a complex process of bullying on a grand and subtle scale. Sometimes Wiliam feels damned if he does, damned if he doesn't. He considers for a long time how best to stand up to this persecution without venting anger and aggression, without becoming defensive, passive or cowed. He finds a way in stillness, which cannot be mis-interpreted or contrived. He prays regularly and deeply.

The church-goers hobby then is Wiliam's character assassination. They gnash their teeth and grind their jaws, taking any opportunity to insult the farmer and his family. His criticism of Vicar John Owen's sermon in Llanarmon churchyard becomes a story of hostile defiance. Owen uses it as evidence of a serious insult and challenge to his honour.

One night the vicar Edward Nanney – the same man who has presided over the Prichard family's marriages and funerals – forces his way into Glasfrynfawr, drunk and abusive. They struggle to get him out of the door before Wiliam finally manhandles him out. This episode forms more ammunition for the malicious Anglican clergy, proving that Wiliam is not only morally corrupt, but violent too.

Vicar Owen's reports are relayed to Wiliam's landlord and owner of Glasfrynfawr, Mr Lloyd. Wiliam's neighbour at Glasfrynbach, a little old lady he has been on perfectly good terms with up until now, says that Wiliam has cut down wood on Mr Lloyd's land. She swears that this is true – it isn't, but provides the final straw needed for Mr Lloyd to give Wiliam notice of eviction.

The kitchen school is disbanded, Jenkin Morgan is arrested and sent from gaol to gaol as a common tramp, back to the south from whence he came, and Wiliam and his family are hounded out of Glasfrynfawr.

Penmynydd

1741

Twelve-year-old Huw rides in the front cart with his dad, and Jane follows closely behind with the girls – Elin, Margaret, Mary and baby Jane. They are riding out of Pen Llŷn to his wife's home country, the island of Ynys Môn. Jane hasn't spoken much, the children haven't spoken much, they are all just following him, relying on him.

They follow the road out of Pen Llŷn, along the coast towards Caernarfon. Shafts of sunlight illuminate occasional patches of sea and the broad back of Ynys Enlli. A shifting beam momentarily glances Garn Ganol on his left, creating an intense triangular accent of green.

From the summit of Garn Ganol you can see anyone, or anything, coming for miles around – the distant line of the Wicklow hills, Holy Island and Llanddwyn sands yellow at the mouth of the Menai Straits, the place to which they are now heading.

Wiliam has climbed these mountains with John many times, imagining the ancients who lived there two thousand years ago, in the Iron Age settlement of Tre'r Ceiri – hunters, fishermen, messengers who formed links and connections between each iconic place, protecting their own land.

Two thousand years ago – Wiliam knows that this particular time, here, now, holding the reins, is a tiny fraction of a much greater whole. He tells himself this, riding forward grimly, the reeds by the side of the road stained red ochre at the base, contrasting with tips of otherworldly lime.

He and John used to camp by a cairn on top of Garn Ganol, a sheltered spot where they sat on sheer rock. There was no rabbit, no sheep, only furry lichen and spent bilberry bushes. He knows this landscape in an intimate way – his ancestors are all buried here. They, like him, knew the make-up, nature, shapes and forms of this country. You know a land more by walking it – the details become familiar, help us to recognise and remember, placing the landscape in both our geographical and psychic memory map.

Wiliam feels himself being pulled out of Llŷn as a long thorn, pulled out of the ground, leaves a hole, raw and seemingly impossible to heal – but knows it will be quickly lawned over by the comfortable certitude of the establishment, so that it may be as though he was never there at all.

To reach their new home on the island of Môn Wiliam and his family cross the Menai Strait, the channel of sea which separates the island from the mainland. It is only a narrow crossing, perhaps a mile across from Y Felinheli to Llanedwen, but the different tidal pulls at each end of the straits make it particularly treacherous.

Disembarking at Llanedwen they ride inland, seagulls wheeling in the low band of sunlight as they reach Penmynydd, to begin the long downhill to the Plas. In the hedgerow hawthorn berries are intense concentrations of red, their hardness a premonition of the winter to come.

Prior to Wiliam's arrival on the island Vicar John Owen has distributed a printed pamphlet around Ynys Môn, as a way of making sure that Wiliam's reputation – as a dangerous man with a strange new religion – has preceded him.

Know that from Glasfryn in Eifionydd, Caernarfonshire
comes one Wiliam Prichard to Penmynydd Anglesey,
who is the first Teacher of this heretical Sect in our land
and from his sour apple-tree grow these three branches
whose fruits are so frequent, namely Methodists, Dis-
senters (or Nonconformists), and Moravians.

The stone walls of Plas Penmynydd are the colour of old tea, the building so steeped in history it looks as if it's having trouble wringing it all out. The Plas has a royal pedigree, from thirteenth-century links to Llywelyn the Great, to the fifteenth-century Harri ap Tudur, whose name was Anglicized to Henry Tudor. Crowned King of England in 1485, Henry VII reigned for twenty-four years.

Alongside the main house are barns and outbuildings and a short distance in front of the farm is the river Ceint, meandering through the steep valley.

Early the next morning Wiliam walks a long loop from the house, up the road to the other side of the valley, The track that leads you to Plas Penmynydd is the same one that takes you out – it is a cul-de-sac – a haven if you are happy, if you are unhappy, a trap.

As he reaches the main road the horizon widens and he heads downhill, over the bridge that crosses the river then uphill to the other side of the valley, turning right past a farm where a dog barks at him ferociously. There is no sign of the owner and as he passes he wonders whether he is friend or foe.

Leaning on a gate Wiliam looks back across the valley at the Plas on the other side, the windows reflecting the morning light. He feels unnerved, surrounded by acquisitiveness, wondering about fear, territory and ownership.

He thinks about the things that divide, if we let them – religion or language, class, wealth, race, gender, and how humanity and compassion undercuts the lot.

Walking down the steep incline to Llanffinan church, he passes through the gate and over a wooden bridge, the water level low on gravel shingle. As he approaches the Plas his strange uneasiness dissipates – there is no need for any of it. The children are playing in the garden, Huw has set up a rope and Elin and Margaret are using it as a swing. It is an idyll. He glances behind from where he has just come, the church just visible through the trees.

Wiliam is an experienced farmer, with all the livestock, equipment and capital necessary to settle this large farm, but it is not an easy task that he has taken on. Vicar John Owen has made sure that his new neighbours view him with deep suspicion and outright hostility. As yet, his new landlord, the Reverend John Edmunds, is on good terms with him – but Owen is working hard to smear Wiliam's name wherever he can.

Owen's parishioners have been told that to trade with Wiliam, indeed even to hold a *conversation* with him will lead to certain derangement, such is the nature of his dangerous new religion. So from the very beginning everyone looks at the family as though they have the plague.

A passing drover turns his sheep onto Wiliam's land, damaging the remaining harvest. Wiliam and his men try to turn them off, but are shot at in the fields. Wiliam practices forebearance, and demands his family and workers do the same, meaning they do not retaliate.

One morning in January he wakes later than usual. Sounds are subdued and the kitchen is a tone darker, where snow has settled on the windowpane. Throughout the day temperatures drop well below zero, the easterly gales forming drifts and whirling around the corners of the house, making it difficult to catch your breath.

Over the following weeks there is no significant further snowfall, but the ground is frozen solid, the sunlight bouncing white, creating a landscape of immaculate splendour. How you expend your energy in these conditions becomes a considered, measured thing. The wind is so cold they cannot speak as they go about their chores, collecting fuel for the stove, feeding themselves and the starving cattle.

When the patches of ice thaw a little the sheep graze on meagre patches of scorched grass – but the thaw is short-lived, the sun so low in the sky. When the ice eventually does melt it becomes apparent how much damage has been done, how blasted the land has been by the arctic temperatures.

By the end of March they are struggling to get by. April finds them pulling straw from the rooves of the barns to feed the animals in an attempt to keep them alive – even so, a third of the cattle and horses die. Some neighbouring families abandon their farms altogether in the face of such hardship. Wiliam uses all his resources just to pull them through that first winter, one of the hardest the island has ever known.

Blackthorn

At the brow of Penmynydd the view opens up to the mountains in the distance, the cloudscapes drape and lift in receding layers across Yr Wyddfa, Carneddau and Yr Eifl.

Around the Plas the blackthorn blossoms, fallen petals cream in brown puddles. Everything about blackthorn is awkward, resilient – they are threadbare yet give rise to this froth, this transformation. It is as though all year they are deliberately obstinate, before deciding to delight. The essence of what it is that makes tiny flowers, lying dormant all winter, deep in the ground, now explodes, forming a bridal column that crowns the day.

As the blackthorn fades in its place comes a new force – stronger, altogether greener. As the old blossom leaves centre stage, the new hawthorn leaves fill the gap seamlessly.

In the shining field there are pink tips on closing daisies, the bluebells in the grove are an intoxication of blue. The ploughed field is a dark burgundy where the shadows fall and light above, the lines receding into the distance. The pale stony earth along the edge of the field is cracked, the colour of clouds.

Over time word gets around the island that, contrary to Vicar Owen's warnings, Wiliam Prisiart is a perfectly regular man. Gradually over the next couple of years the island community get to know him, and not all of them are set against him.

There are three brothers from Tŷ Gwyn who have started to join him when he rides the forty miles to Llangybi each month, to meet Francis, Lewis and the others at Capel Helyg. The brothers and Wiliam begin to meet in each other's houses, registering their meeting place with the Spiritual Court.

One of the brothers, Henry, manages to register his home in Cerrigceinwen and they begin to plan a school there. Jenkin Morgan, released from gaol, joins them and together they form an independent congregation at Henry's house.

As the services get bigger they move from Henry's house to Minffordd, a cottage closer to Penmynydd that

Wiliam has managed to register. They invite Lewis Rees to preach here and he rides up in July.

News of Lewis Rees' visit sweeps through the district and about fifty people come to listen to his sermon at Minffordd, some of them from Capel Helyg, some of them Wiliam's new neighbours.

There is another gang of about a dozen men hanging around the sidelines, who seem intent on disrupting things, but Wiliam's worst fears are not realised.

Everything quietens down when Rees begins to speak – in fact the entire congregation are completely silent, transfixed by Lewis Rees as though by an angel. They hold another service in the afternoon but this time that small group manage to disrupt it to such an extent that they have to abandon it.

Over the last couple of years Vicar John Owen has moved swiftly up the ecclesiastical ranks, from vicar to canon and now chancellor of Bangor Cathedral, a role of great power and authority.

Owen's appointment comes as something as a surprise to many of his peers, who question the bishop's judgement in appointing someone so well-known for his litigious temper.

One morning in August a church court official appears at Plas Penmynydd and hands Wiliam a piece of paper.

The Office against William Prichard of
Penmynydd, Yeoman.
To answer to Articles which shall be objected against
him touching his Soul's health and
reformation of his Manners and more especially for
Scandalizing and Defaming the Officiating Minister at
the parish Church of Llannor in the County of Carnarvon

The summons requires Wiliam to appear in the Spiritual Court in Bangor Cathedral to answer to these crimes. Vicar John Owen has bided his time until he is in a truly powerful position before bringing a legal case against him and as Chancellor of Bangor Cathedral, Owen is effectively judge and jury.

Wiliam seeks legal advice, but struggles to find a decent lawyer. Eventually he finds one who is prepared to defend him, who explains that the foundation of the case is based on his 'inappropriate attitude' towards the Church of England. This is evidenced by Wiliam's public criticism of the chancellor's sermon three years ago at Llannor churchyard. The reason they can bring a case against him at all is that he criticised the Chancellor *whilst still on church grounds.*

Wiliam has no choice but to appear in the Spiritual Courts to argue his case, in a grim pantomime which rolls on month by month – sometimes the chancellor shows up in the cathedral court, sometimes he doesn't. The case rumbles on in a circular farce, the lawyer needing money up front with no visible progress, so that financial ruin looks increasingly likely – excactly, in fact, what Owen intends for the farmer and his family.

Riot

1742

The hawthorn trees along the wall are green-gold, strangely lit in an otherwise sodden day. All around the clouds are charcoal grey, but the hawthorn's complicated branches are infused with light, though there is no sun to be seen.

Enlightened, they are saturated in this one-colour channel – green-gold, or gold-green. It is as though the light emanates from within the trees themselves, although of course this cannot be.

Wiliam leans against Minffordd's door, knocks again and tries the handle, but finds it locked. He looks around at the gathering crowd. There are about fifteen men nearby, most of them tenant farmers – except for Hywel Tŷ Gwyn, hardly one of them owns his own place. Hywel is joined by his two brothers Henry and Thomas, their wives, servants and neighbouring families.

Francis Caertyddyn and many of the Capel Helyg congregation have come up from Llangybi, so there are about two hundred people gathered for the service. As they cannot access the house, Wiliam asks Jenkin to take the service out here in the field.

Seen from above, the cloud shadows shift so quickly over the landscape – across the mill, farm, gorse and heather. The sky is a vast arc, the animated figures below concentrated stitches in a giant unfolding weave. In the dun fields, flocks of starlings are unremarkable until they rise.

Jenkin steps onto a wooden stand, his voice competing with the wind that runs through the trees, whisking up the broad leaves which flap this way and that.

Along the fringes of the crowd a group of men have begun to cluster. They encircle Jenkin on his low platform, heckling him.

'Under whose authority are you here?'

Peter, the curate of Llanffinan church, shouts loudly and officiously.

Jenkin pauses in his sermon and the congregation wait expectantly as he fishes out a piece of paper, which he holds out to the curate.

'Protestant Dissenting Teacher who is duly and
properly qualified to Preach the Gospel according to the
Laws in that Case made and Provided'

The licence proves Jenkin Morgan's legal entitlement to be there, and makes absolutely no difference to the curate, who dismisses it derisively, slicing his arm through the air. It is an incisive gesture, one that frames the outcome of the day. Until that moment there is a sort of equilibrium, the shouts and heckles just a ragged accompaniment to the preacher, almost lost in the wide air.

In the gesture of the raised arm, hatred coalesces to a focal point. Every element holds still just for a second, time suspended as they all look at it, this potent threat. It is as though everything now awakens, the clarity of adrenalin blowing any uncertainty away.

What follows then is chaotic. The crowd shudder as the pack drag Jenkin from his stand and set upon him with their clubs and staves. The congregation scatter, fleeing from the fracas at the same time as the church sexton runs towards it, cudgel in hand.

Wiliam and the others have no defence against their iron-tipped clubs and shield their heads as best they can. Their ideology upholds non-violence, so Wiliam offers no resistance as the blows rain down on him, one particular blow so hard that the iron spike breaks clean away from the club, into the side of his head.

They are pursued, crushed and beaten for more than a quarter of a mile, so much so that the road streams with their blood. Still offering no resistance, Wiliam and the others walk slowly, as though they were mules, vilified every step of the way.

They dare not go to their own homes and decide instead to walk directly to the house of the local Justice of the Peace, to make an account of what has just happened. The servant who answers the doors tells them the Judge is not at home.

'He's sure to be here tomorrow, why don't you come back then?'

So Wiliam and others spend the night at houses other than their own, and return the next morning to see the Judge.

'You've just missed him'.

They show their wounds and recount the tale, but it all seems ineffectual somehow – deliberately so, Wiliam thinks, as he and Jenkin ride the route home to Plas Penmynydd.

He leans against the window in the front room, in the half-light of the late autumn afternoon. Starlings alight in the uppermost part of the ash tree, indistinguishable from the leaves until they take flight, one by one in different directions. Lower down, two ravens sit steady – a treble and a bass clef. When they fly away their croak is distinct, the broad span of their wings black against the lighter clouds.

Rooks, their legs as thin as the twigs on which they perch, grasp onto the highest branches. They sway, wings folded to their bodies, balancing in the wind, they are ships at sea, sailors in a storm. Their claws hold them tight, the weight of their bodies seeming to contradict the possibility of it at all. They seem perfectly at home, occasionally rising to hover, wingtips upturned, frayed edges holding them afloat until they alight somewhere lower.

The turbulent sky has torn ribbons of brown and pink clouds, a promise to the west as the sun sets. There is clarity to every line of the ash, backlit by the sunset. As though magnetised to the blowing boughs, the rooks rest tenaciously on the furthest outpost branches.Wind-blasted, it is a tempest and they ride it. Separate, together, a loose gang, strung out.

The starlings roost in a city of chatter, a junction of news and responses, they rise together as one as the last drabs of light are spent, there is that iridescent lime blue as the sun sinks and soon the trees will be indistinguishable from the winter sky.

Raid

1743

'What do you mean, pray for him – you're joking, right?'

Jane thinks it is psychological cruelty being meted out to them by Chancellor Owen and his like.

Owen is the instigator, she knows, and he is trying to systematically destroy them, their reputations and livelihood. So the idea that she should *pray* for this man seems an outrage to her, and she says as much to her husband.

But praying for him is exactly what Wiliam is doing. The effects of the chancellor's words and deeds are so insulting, so upsetting that they enrage him – when this happens and he is in a fine state of emotion, Wiliam directs every ounce of his energy into prayer for the man.

In the same way that he heard Francis praying for his

neighbours that night through the window, Wiliam focuses the same simple feeling of peace to the man that is trying to destroy him.

'His hatred is just a sign of his fear or losing control, of his insecurity. We have to find another way, something other than meeting hatred with hatred,' he says.

'But he's a total bastard,'

Jane is not wrong. Sometimes as he walks over his fields Wiliam finds words like these slipping out. He hears himself say them, as he reflects on Owen's actions, amazed at the malice of the man. So he focuses even more on countering these unkind thoughts immediately, with sentiments of goodwill. It feels counter-intuitive, but he knows it is the only way that he can deal with it, the only thing that will ultimately bring him peace.

In January Wiliam and Jane christen their new son Rhisiart in Llanffinan church. The name has three different forms, the Welsh *Rhisiart*, Latin *Richardus* and English *Richard*. How it is used depends on whether it is spoken, written and by whom, thinks Wiliam, as 'Richard Williams' is inscribed in Llanffinan church registry.

The law is that all official documentation in Wales is to be in English, which means that the centuries old patronymic naming system is being eroded. In the old patronymic system, each child is given the father's first name as a surname – so Wiliam is named after his father,

Richard Morus. These surnames, which effectively change with each generation will eventually be eradicated, with surnames becoming fixed and Anglicised, and the church christening is an example of that.

Wiliam's own name – *Wiliam ap Rhisiart* – is often anglicised to William Pritchard – with the extra *l* in the forename, the *p* at the start of the surname a remnant of the original *ap,* or 'son of'.

Wiliam's son, Rhisiart ap Wiliam in the old form – becomes Richard Williams, in a mutation that will now become concrete, the old patronymic system giving way to the new, English form.

Morus ap Owen

|

Rhisiart ap Morus

|

William ap Rhisiart

|

Rhisiart ap Wiliam

English has become the compulsory language of law and administration throughout Wales – which is fine for the English-speaking Welsh gentry – less so for the working class. Around ninety percent of people in Wales don't understand the English language, so rely heavily on

translation for important legal and administrative matters
– often native Welsh speakers are tried in the courts in a
language they don't understand.

The Welsh gentry – who *do* understand the language
– are thriving, building estates, becoming local governors
and top dogs in society, with a voice at Westminster. As
they become increasingly Anglicised they swap their
Welsh surnames for more English versions – Meurig becomes Meyrick, for example.

A couple of weeks later, on a dull Saturday afternoon
in February, the men who instigated the Minffordd riot
sit around the tavern, cursing Wiliam Prichard and his
family, hatching a new plan to destroy the man.

They set off on horseback around the neighbourhood
gathering information on the 'Roundhead' Wiliam Prichard
and his 'Preacher' Jenkin Morgan and are told that the
two were seen near Pentre Berw earlier that afternoon,
heading for Penmynydd.

The term 'roundhead' has evolved from the English
Civil War, a battle fought a hundred years earlier between
the Parliamentarians ('Roundheads') and Royalists, (or
'Cavaliers') Most Welshmen don't like the revolutionary
ideas of the Parliamentarians, who question the divine
rights of Kings and want to see the establishment of a
constitutional monarchy. Many Puritans and 'Dissenters'
however, support the parliamentarians, largely due to their

more tolerant approach to Independent ideas of worship.

There is another, populist shorthand for these complicated ideologies – puritans generally wear their hair close-cut, giving rise to the term 'Roundhead' in that their hair literally follows the contours of their scalp, in contrast to the long ringlets of the Royalist cavaliers.

In future generations the term 'Roundhead' will be superseded by 'Whig', and 'Cavalier' by 'Tory'. The Whigs will eventually evolve into the Liberal party, but until then representation at Westminster is by landowners and landed gentry – you can only vote if you own land.

The monarchists are fiercely indignant of any perceived slight against 'their' King, making rational progressive debate almost impossible.

Sunday morning dawns overcast and windy at the Plas. Morwynig the maid lights a fire in the front room and this is where Jane sits, nursing the baby Rhisiart. Outside the trees toss in the wind like a wild tide, the window panes rattle in their casings. Morwynig busies in from the kitchen.

'Shall I take him something up?'

Morwynig wipes her hands on her apron. Huw is in bed upstairs, where he has been for the last two weeks, with a running fever.

'Yes, thanks, that would be good. I popped in to see him earlier, but he was flat out'.

'I'll go up in a minute and see how he's doing'

Morwynig picks up Jane's empty teacup, turns away from the fire to the long windows.

'Brenin Mawr!'

Alarmed, Morwynig steps back from the window.

'What is it?'

Jane rises awkwardly with the baby and the two women watch from the cover of the curtains as a crowd of men march into the front yard – a whole phalanx of them, armed with clubs, as though they are an army. There are two hundred of them, many of whom the women recognize – church people, local farmers, the curate Peter leading them.

'What do they want?'

Morwynig is still clutching the teacup, in danger of crushing it.

'Nothing good' says Jane wryly.

The two women confer hurriedly, and Jane retakes her seat by the fire, her back to the window, Rhisiart in her arms. She holds one hand over the other, to stop herself from trembling.

The men who have marched on Penmynydd are all members of the Anglican church. The curate Peter hammers loudly on the door and getting no immediate response he hammers again. After a minute or so the maid Morwynig opens the door.

'Good morning Sir'

'Fetch me your master'

'Who shall I say is calling, please?'

Morwynig is amazed at her own audacity.

'Just get him'

Peter is in no mood for social pleasantries.

'Wiliam Prichard!' he shouts up at the house

'We have come for you!'

Behind him the crowd are lined up shoulder to shoulder.

Morwynnig leaves the door and goes back into the main room, where Jane is waiting.

'Get him a drink' she says in a low voice to Morwynig, rising with the baby still in her arms, walking slowly to the open door.

'Good morning' she greets Peter pleasantly

'How can I help you'

'We have come to kill your husband the Roundhead' shouts Peter.

The crowd behind him roar, raising their clubs, knives and batons into the air.

Jane is framed in the doorway, holding the baby.

'If Roundhead you call him, he is not at home' she says equably

'Could I offer you a drink?'

Right on cue, Morwynig is by her side with a pitcher of ale. Peter takes it and drinks it in one go. Grimacing, he wipes his mouth with his sleeve.

'Are you trying to kill me, woman?'

He snarls at her and holding the pitcher high, he shakes it around, so that Jane can just about hear some loose zinc in the glaze, a small clatter within the ceramic piece.

Peter casts the pitcher behind him, where it cracks and breaks on the ground. The mob cheer.

Peter leans in, his left hand resting on the doorframe, his face right up against Jane's, so that she can smell his breath, see the spittle.

'You're lying' his voice is lower

'We saw them yesterday afternoon, coming here'.

'Well they're not here now' says Jane

'Come inside to look for yourselves if you want' and she stands sideways on, as though to let them pass.

'You people' Peter says 'Vermin' and he spits on the step.

In one move Jane stands back and Morwynig swifly closes the door. Huw is standing on the bottom stair, white as a sheet. The three of them stand in the stairwell, locked in each other's gaze as the baby begins to wail.

They mob flood against the walls of the house, smashing the windows, shattering the glass, distorting the lead casing into angry angles. They run into the barns where they destroy anything they can find, smashing the plough

and kicking the wooden stalls into splinters. In the grana-
ry they mix together the wheat, oats and barley, rendering
them useless.

They shout, curse, damn and condemn – but they
don't come in. Finally, when they have ruined everything
they can find, they leave, a scene of devastation in their
wake.

What Jane says is true – Wiliam and Jenkin are not
at home, having risen extra early to ride to Llangybi for
communion at Capel Helyg. Some of the labourers and
the other children set off for Llanffinan church that morning, so that Jane, Morwynig, Huw and the baby Rhisiart
were indeed the only ones at home.

When Wiliam returns and Jane recounts to her husband all that has happened Wiliam realises that the lives
of his family are in danger, that his patience with these
people has only made them the more cruel and daring.

'What is it with these people?'

Realising that he cannot continue in the same way,
he decides to find some proper legal recourse and swiftly
appoints a new lawyer, one who will represent him in his
battles with Chancellor Owen at the Spiritual Court.

Llanffinan

In March the clouds form a blanket over the sun. There are rooks, seagulls and dandelions on the track down to Llanffinan church. The cherry tree is just beginning to bud and Wiliam feels large and clumsy treading on the primroses as they bury Huw.

In the following months Wiliam is bound in a terrible cycle of despair, questioning his loss constantly, finding no answer. He wakes in the night with a hammering heart, which continues throughout the day as he tries to find some meaning in it. He fixates on disparate events of his son's life, running over and over Huw's history and character. He spends weeks in this state, searching for reasons, replaying snatches of imagery.

On an afternoon in August he finds himself sitting

with his mother-in-law in the garden, trying to put his confusion into words. He hears himself in the telling, as he watches a dandelion head float down, a golden orb hovering about a foot away from him at eye level. It moves directly towards him, so that he finds his sad words slowing and trailing away to a halt. Lit by the late afternoon sun, he is transfixed, instantly conscious that he can now let go.

At night the peace of this simple moment stays with him. He remembers Christ and lets him in to that space of pain, somewhere in his solar plexus. He lets him in to fill it, because nothing else can. And it is as though, once invited, Christ takes that central space seamlessly, without a murmur. There is no turmoil, no upheaval, but all the grief and anxiety is no longer his alone.

He has someone working on his side, so that he may not always be aware of it, and certainly not understand it, but the centre of his body is healed and will continue to heal, with every breath he takes.

Wiliam gives the names of all the men involved in the riots, the beatings, ransacking and raid on the Plas to his new lawyer, who wastes no time in raising the existing case of Chancellor Owen against William Prichard out of the Spiritual Courts to the Great Sessions in Beaumaris, where it is promptly settled in Wiliam's favour.

'You could have him thrown out, you know'

His lawyer advises him, packing away his papers at the conclusion of the trial. Should he decide to press charges, Wiliam would be successful and Chancellor Owen would lose his position. Wiliam deliberates over this for a week or so, knowing that his actions now could destroy Owen's career – indeed, his whole sense of being. He feels this victory as a great responsibility and ultimately decides against pressing charges. It is enough, he thinks, that he has proved his case, and that the matter is now ended.

Having won the legal battle many of Wiliam's enemies are now much more careful, fearing the long arm of the law will reach them. The fury of Chancellor Owen, however, is in no way diminished. Having lost the case, Owen is unable to let it go and avenges himself by forming whatever damaging stories he can think of about Wiliam. With his friends, landowners Owen Morris and Viscount Bulkeley, they tell Wiliam's landlord that his tenant has brought destructive heresies to the island and that he has been encouraging men to revolt against the King. Wiliam's landlord, not wanting to harbour a dangerous heretic, decides to evict Wiliam and his family from Plas Penmynydd.

Llanddaniel
1745

Wiliam feels as though some thing, some bone in his head, has broken. He carries a blackthorn walking-stick, his palm cupped over the small metal plate set into the handle. The stick looks perfectly innocuous, but a flick of his thumb triggers a mechanism which moves the plate and reveals a six-inch metal spike housed within. This cane and a large hound are his protection as he goes around the island looking for a new home.

There are four roads leading out of the centre of Llanddaniel. The road south runs past Bodlewfawr, a farmhouse facing east across the Menai Strait to Eryri and the long arm of the Llŷn peninsula. Wiliam secures tenancy of Bodlew and they move in the September.

Not long after they have settled in a young man

comes to the house with the express intention of killing Wiliam. He is part of the gang who gather in the pubs of Caernarfon, men who have spent many hours gnawing at Wiliam's reputation, for 'subverting innocent people', disowning the church and so on.

The intruder enters Bodlew armed with a knife bought from Caernarfon especially for the job. He finds the family gathered together in the house, deep in prayer and is struck by the simple proof of their belief.

'Good God,' he mutters, 'if that is how he prays, I am not going to harm the man,' and leaves, pocketing the knife as he goes.

On market day Wiliam takes the cattle on the ferry from Llanedwen across to Caernarfon. After the market he has a bite in the pub, groaning when he realises Owen Paradwys and his gang are there too.

A strong Anglican landowner, Paradwys is known as the 'Giant of the World'. They heckle Wiliam while he bolts his lunch, escapes the pub and makes his way back to the ferry, for the short return journey across the water back to the island.

Owen Paradwys is on the same barge and Wiliam feels sure something is brewing, though the journey passes peacefully enough, the barge making it's way evenly across the water, the horses calm and steady.

As they approach the quay at Llanedwen Paradwys

spots his advantage. Wiliam's horse is spooked by the idling boat, so Wiliam stands at it's head, holding the bridle, trying to calm it. Raising his stick Paradwys thrashes Wiliam's horse so that it rears, rocking the ferry and putting all the passengers in immediate danger.

'Stop! What are you doing, man?' Wiliam shouts, hanging on to the bridle.

'Quiet you, you Roundhead or I will beat you too,' snarls Paradwys, striking out at Wiliam with the stick.

The ferry draws alongside the quay and Wiliam leads his horse carefully onto dry land. Safely on shore he turns to face Paradwys.

'What in God's name are you doing? Why are you beating my horse, for no reason?'

Paradwys' answer is full of profanities. He sets to beating Wiliam about the head with his stick. Wiliam drops the reins and rushes at Paradwys, tackling him about the knees and knocking the big man flat. He grabs hold of his feet and drags him along the road, the gravel tearing mercilessly into his clothes and flesh.

'Murder! Murder! In the name of God, save me!' The passengers, now safely disembarked, look on, but not one of them lifts a finger to help him.

When they hear the 'Giant of the World' has lost the fight, the Caernarfon gang don't pose any problems to Wiliam ever again. The young man with the knife has been telling his story of redemption in every pub in Caernarfon, and ordinary people begin to see he is more like them than not. They realise that the rumours surrounding Wiliam are unfounded, and so the sting goes out of his persecution.

Although the Caernarfon gang are leaving him alone, however, the church are still firmly set against him. The Independent movement is gathering momentum, with people leaving the Anglican church in their droves, choosing instead to listen to the Nonconformist preachers, and new meeting houses are being registered in Cerrigceinwen, Tŷ Gwyn and Llanddaniel for this purpose.

As the free schools become established alongside the religious services, confidence in the movement grows. At the same time, a schism develops, between the Nonconformist and Methodist movements. Methodism is different from – but importantly still a part of – the Church of England, whereas Wiliam, Jenkin and the Nonconformists want to distance themselves entirely from the church.

Up until now, the Methodists and Nonconfomists have had a friendly and supportive relationship, often sharing meetingplaces. Now however, on behalf of the Methodist movement, Howel Harris is sent up to the island to try to calm the waters a bit, meeting Wiliam, Jenkin and a large audience in the Llanddaniel meeting house. He begins his speech, trying to ameliorate the crowd.

'You have the liberty to dissent in a spiritual way, but don't distance yourself so obviously – so visibly – from the church,' he implores them.

'Don't leave the established church entirely, rather continue to take communion within the Anglican church, so as not to risk ex-communication'

Harris is seeking to convince them to maintain the current state of duality, and Wiliam feels sad and uneasy. He doesn't understand how Harris can argue his case, knowing the man's strong beliefs – why would he ever champion such a compromise? The crowd are in uproar.

'You are a deceiver!'

Harris is getting heckled – somebody from the back shouts, and as Harris looks around it occurs to him that the Nonconformists will take every last person away from the Anglican church.

Wiliam, Jenkin Morgan, Daniel Rowland try to convince Harris and the Methodists to leave the Anglican church themselves, and the meeting dissolves into angry disagreement. After this, the Methodists decide not to allow the Nonconformists to preach in their societies any longer, putting a stop to the friendly arrangement that has been in place up until now.

The schism causes the Nonconformists, led by Daniel Rowlands, to branch off from the Methodists, who continue to follow Harris.

Notwithstanding these tensions, the Nonconformist movement is burgeoning, and Chancellor Owen and his friends continue to look for new and ingenious ways to bring about Wiliam's downfall.

They pick on any opportunity to disrupt his home and livelihood. One evening two constables appear at Bodlewfawr with a warrant for the arrest of Morus Griffith, Wiliam's labourer and a man of outstanding piety. One constable enters the house and the other waits outside, to make sure the young man doesn't make a run for it.

The constable comes into the kitchen, where Morus is sitting with the other labourers at the kitchen table.

'Well, you can't take him just like that,' says Jane, facing the constable with her back to the stove, hands on her hips.

'The poor lad's still eating his supper. At least let him go upstairs and put something on his feet.'

'Alright, he can do that,' agrees the constable. 'It'll make it easier for him to walk to Beaumaris gaol.'

So up the stairs goes Morus, and away through the garret window, across the fields at the back of the farm, down to the Menai's edge.

Stymied by these escapades, the churchmen persevere. When all else fails, they resort to tried and tested methods. Discovering that Wiliam's landlady at Bodlew is the daughter of the Reverend John Ellis, they lean on him, so that the reverend strongly advises his daughter to get rid of her tenant, the Nonconformist troublemaker. She duly gives Wiliam six months to clear out, and so the family are once more evicted from their home.

Cnwchdernog
1749

Wiliam can't find anywhere to live on Ynys Môn, nor in the neighbouring county. Finally he hears that the judge, William Bulkeley has three smallholdings to let in the north of the island. On a sunny day in late February, with a brisk southeasterly breeze, Wiliam rides out to the landowner's home at Brynddu, finding the judge cocooned in his study.

Bulkeley asks him general questions about his farming – how many head of cattle does he have, how much acreage does he currently farm? With each answer the judge becomes increasingly curious as to why this man, with so much capital and experience, is looking for somewhere anew.

'Why is it that you are leaving the place you are at

the moment – can't you afford the rent?' Bulkeley asks.

'No, it's nothing like that,' says Wiliam.

'It's because I am a Nonconformist, a Dissenter from the English church.'

Bulkeley raises his eyebrows. 'Well, if they haven't got anything worse than that to say about you, I can give you enough land.'

The two men ride up to the three farms – Cnwchdernog Uchaf, Cnwchdernog Croes and Cnwchdernog Isaf. The buildings are dilapidated, but Bulkeley agrees to fix the hedges along the perimeters, the cowshed and barn, as well as making good the house, repairing windows and so on. Back in the study at Brynddu they agree on a rent of fifty pounds a year, on a twenty-one year lease.

'It's none of my business, of course.' says Bulkeley mildly, as they shake hands.

'But I can't help but think it would be better for you to agree with the Anglican church.'

On All Hallows' Eve that year Wiliam, Jane and their seven children – Elin, Margaret, Mary, Jane, Rhisiart, Catherine and the new baby, John – move into Cnwchdernog.

Over the following years a friendship develops between Wiliam and the judge. Alhough not a Dissenter himself, it gives Bulkeley a particular pleasure to see the irritation of his fellow gentlemen when he meets them in the Bulls' Head, after the Quarter Sessions in Beaumaris. 'They are religiously mad, I tell you!' the viscount expostulates over his brandy.

'Just a couple of years ago this island was almost entirely Church of England – now it's full of Methodists, or Independents, or Presbyterians, or some other sect – God knows what they're called – I don't think they know themselves.'

They tread warily around Bulkeley, as he is effectively harbouring the Nonconformist leader, but none of them are in a position to take issue with him, and can't for the life of them understand why he has taken on such a controversial tenant.

Wiliam registers Cnwchdernog as an Independent meeting place and they begin to hold regular services there, with visiting ministers from across the country, including John Wesley.

Although he has had a lot of communication with the London Dissenters, he has never met Wesley up until now and is pleased at the prospect, inviting him to stay over on his way to the ferry at Holyhead. The organised London Dissenters' support has been invaluable to Wiliam, helping him both legally and financially when he was at his lowest point, saving him, in fact, from going under, in the case with Chancellor Owen.

Wesley arrives at Cnwchdernog on the last Saturday

in March and on the Sunday preaches to a large congregation of Wiliam's friends and neighbours, including Thomas Williams from Pentre Bwaau.

'Lay not up for yourselves treasures upon earth.'

Wesley has the crowd captivated, as he explores themes of wealth and poverty, suggesting the 'primitive' peoples of Africa and the Americas have a greater grasp of what is spiritually civilised than those who call themselves Christian. He lays out complicated themes so simply, thinks Wiliam, his argument laying bare contemporary hypocrisy.

'If you add house to house and field to field – why do you call yourself Christian?'

After the sermon, many of Wiliam's guests from the nearby town of Llannerch-y-medd beseech Wesley to preach there. Wesley doesn't refuse, but in conversation with Wiliam later that evening he confesses his reservations, thinking that not all his listeners will be sympathetic to his ideas.

The next day they go to the friend's house in town, to preach there, but Wesley has scarcely sat down before a gang of men gather outside, shouting oaths and curses in broad Welsh.

Wiliam and the others entreat Wesley to stay safely indoors, but Wesley thinks it best to look the crowd straight in the eye, whilst it is still daylight. He makes them open the door and preaches on the doorstep to the people of Llannerch-y-medd.

'The vast majority of rich men are under a peculiar curse, Not only are they corrupting their own souls, they're also robbing the poor, the hungry and making themselves accountable for all the affliction and distress which they could – but do not – remove.'

It is difficult to hear him over the shouts and heckling.

'Does not the blood of all those who perish for want of what the rich either lay up or lay out needlessly, does not their blood cry out against the rich, from the earth?'

The crowd's Welsh curses are lost upon Wesley, as his language is upon them.

Rhosmeirch

Wiliam and Jane have three more children at Cnwchdernog – Evan, William and finally, when Jane is forty-eight,
their last son, Dafydd.

At the same time as the family is growing, so are the
ambitions of the Nonconformists, so much so that in 1748
Wiliam and his friends set about building an Independent
chapel at Rhosmeirch, the first of it's kind on Anglesey.

They file all the necessary legal papers and eventually
achieve the relevant permissions. Construction gets under
way slowly but routinely, so that work progresses, whatever else may be happening.

They level the ground on site and secure upright col-
umns, the wood shining against the dark green trees around
it, which shift and whisper in the breeze. The structure

stands unmoving, establishing itself in this place that they have found. Once the building is clad, never again will you see this underlying structure, this careful and concise arrangement. The parallels and joins are underpinned by a mathematical precision which make it an immovable force.

The A-frames are fixed at thirty-five degree angles. A low triangle, constructed on the ground, when raised up they suddenly define the interior space, which suddenly looks much bigger than they thought it would.

Wiliam stands on the flat ground within the framework. It is different to, yet in sympathy with, the field and the trees. Already it has a sense of 'inside' and 'outside', even though it is all still just air, the upright posts divide lines in space. Invulnerable to wind and storms, the uprights do not move, but stay firm.

Over the following weeks and months they are added to, so that gradually the building becomes established. The birds become familiarised with it as it settles into its rightful place.

Wiliam stands in this space and imagines all the things which will happen in it. They work systematically on the ground, the walls, the roof, doors and windows. The building is so well made that all you have to think about is the play of the breeze in the leaves of the trees, the cast of light and the passing moment.

This chapel's position in the centre of the island is a symbol of its place at the very heart of the community. All the houses Wiliam has lived in on the island – Plas Penmynydd, Bodlewfawr in Llanddaniel, Cnwchdernog in Llanddeusant – are situated around it in a rough triangle, the chapel at the centre.

As different workers appear on the site they bring stories from around the island. Wiliam hears that in south Wales, Howel Harris has set up a religious community in his home town of Trefeca, with himself as the driving force.

'Teulu Trefeca' make everything themselves – their own clothes, food and entertainment. They call Harris 'Father', and the local population are scandalised over this alternative community, and in particular Harris' relationship with his benefactor, Madam Griffith.

He hears strange anecdotes of his adversary Chancellor Owen – of the Chancellor's horse, stalling at a gate, causing Owen to go flying. And more serious rumours – that Owen's Oxford degree is bogus – that the man isn't really who he purports to be. Doubt is cast on his background and integrity.

Chancellor Owen has been demoted within the church, cast out from the glamour of Bangor cathedral to an outlying parish in the north of the island. Wiliam wonders at how the tables turn, how one so feared can be reduced. In 1755 his old adversary Chancellor Owen dies ignominiously, age fifty-seven.

Green Gold

1772

The independent schools continue to proliferate, rising to thirty-seven schools, fifty, then a hundred as the Nonconformist movement spreads throughout the island.

Over the next twenty years their life at Cnwchdernog becomes very peaceful, the meetings no longer disrupted as in the old days. The children grow and move into homes of their own, Rhisiart marries Margaret, the daughter of his old friend Thomas at Pentre Bwaau. None of them are very far away and the younger sons – Evan, Wiliam and Dafydd are still at home, as Wiliam mellows into his seventies.

They lose their youngest, Dafydd, on the last day of March 1771. He is twelve years old.

Later that year Wiliam walks to the henhouse to collect the eggs. There are three, two still warm. His head aches as he bends to pick them up from within the mucky straw. The pain above his eyes means it hurts every time he moves his head. He moves slowly, putting the eggs in his pocket carefully. His hair sticks to his head – hot, cold, damp, he does not know which.

He stands by the henhouse door to get his breath back. Everything drips, but is still. Sounds are muted, but echo. He is dressed, which is an accomplishment, he thinks. His clothes feel as though they are wrapped around a husk. He is concave. Everything in him aches.

And, somehow, in the short time that he's been standing there, the fog has lifted and the sunlight has made green-gold lozenges of the fields around him.

The birdsong is cutting bright, the raindrops shimmer on the leaves in the gentlest breeze. The air is warm, sweet with the smell of hay and apples. He breathes in the sense of fulfilment and possibility and turns to look around, in wonder, that it has changed so quickly. He still can't see the mountains, so perhaps it was just this island, just now, that was scooped out of the mist, to reveal its emerald and azure.

He walks back up the path into the house, as the light changes again, the clouds roll in, the wind picks up and it is a little less uncommon.

At night, there is a noise which comes from deep within him. It is involuntary – you could not call it a cough, it is not exact enough for that. It is more a gruff honk, a hollow bark. It comes frequently, and completely unexpectedly. It feels like it emanates more from his stomach, rather than the chest. It frightens him, this noise, and he goes from his bed in the night, to save waking Jane. He lies awake with a blanket on the kitchen floor with the candle lit, he feels safer that way.

For weeks Wiliam is in the grip of a terrible fever, which tries to steal away his peace of mind. His heart begins to falter – sometimes he falls, and it is a shock, but he keeps on getting up.

When Rhisiart next rides over from Pentre Bwaau Jane asks her son to look through the paperwork, to make sure everything is in order. Rhisiart sifts through a pile of folios and thumbs a small hardback book on top of them, the cherry red cover frayed at the edges. The pages look like mottled, ancient maps. He flicks through the pages, containing meticulously itemised lists of their everyday household expenses.

'*am olchi dillad yr eglwys*' – washing church clothes – features on each page.

The parchment is dry as bone, the calligraphy leaning to the right in his dad's even, measured hand.

'*am olchi dillad yr eglwys*'

'am fund i'r corecsiwn'

'am arch Gruffydd Evan'.

The lists are familiar, the letterforms so tight as to be nearly illegible. In the folios there are letters from the London Dissenters, the immaculate letters forming artistic patterns on the page, the descenders of the 'g' and the ascenders of 'd' and 'f' creating circular motifs. The papers are in tones of muted blue, with the occasional scarlet seal, the wax long since cracked.

He unfolds and flattens the long lists written on the backs of old envelopes.

'Bara'r cymun' – communion bread.

'Gwin' – wine.

Wiliam's more recent handwriting is tiny, the lines going right to the edges of the page, with no margins to speak of. This is in contrast to letters from his friends, one in particular a glorious extravagant scrawl.

There are letters from his brother John, enthusing about painting, with recipes for pigments and diagrams of colour theory. There is paperwork from the court cases, letterheads from High Holborn and London lawyers on thick yellowed paper.

Rhisiart lays the papers flat on the desk – he has spent most of the afternoon looking through them and feels like he has lived through a hundred years. He feels a strange intimacy, an unsettling juxtaposition of the important and the mundane. Outside the day has shifted and he gathers his things.

'I'll be back tomorrow' he kisses his mum and sets off home for Pentre Bwaau.

'How is he?' his father-in-law, Thomas asks him, back in the kitchen at Pentre.

Rhisiart shakes his head

'Not good.'

He can't tell him how thin his dad has become, how his bones ache just lying in bed, the pupils of his eyes so dark.They sit in silence for a while.

Thomas shakes his head

'You know,' he says, 'your dad was a hell of a man. So bloody righteous, my heart would sink if I saw him coming towards me on the road.'

He chuckles, folding his hands.

'I dreaded meeting him – I would be quaking in my boots, as though he could look straight through me, and see all my sins.'

Thomas smiles

'I was scared to meet him, yet at the same time I loved him more than any other neighbour.'

Rhisiart visits Cnwchdernog more frequently now, as they slip into the new year. By February Wiliam's legs won't work, his eyesight has all but gone, he cannot read, clothe nor feed himself and relies on Jane in all things.

Being so dependent can only sadden and frustrate him, but his tenacity is breathtaking, his patience immense. It is clear that only spirit is sustaining him, Rhisiart thinks, as he sits by the bed, reading aloud.

'Father, the hour has come.'

Wiliam clasps a small wooden cross tightly to his chest. He cries out loud sometimes, about devils trying to claim him. Rhisiart calms him, his brave dad, who in his life has never been afraid of anyone or anything.

Inbetween these disturbing bouts Wiliam might sit up in bed and look quite cheerful, his face smooth, his mind once more intact. In one of these moments he asks Rhisiart to gather the family to him – Jane and the children Elin, Margaret, Mary, Jane, Rhisiart, Catherine, John, Evan and William.

'Jane!' Wiliam says, as though he is just seeing her anew, and Rhisiart is awed at the depth and clarity in his dad's voice, how he is holding it together even now, as though this were a regular family meeting.

'I am going to leave you now. I have prayed a lot, for God to show you the way. I haven't seen it up to now – only the smallest sign that He is listening and answering my prayers. It may be, when I am gone, that God will be with you.'

He holds each of their hands, calls them each by name with that same, delighted quality.

'Have faith,' he whispers. 'Trust in His love and goodness.'

Then he says a prayer, and they all bow their heads.

'Oh God, give your grace to my wife and children, so that they can know Jesus Christ married to their souls, and be faithful in your service until death.'

Then Wiliam slips into a sort of slumber. Approaching death, it is as though all the spirit of his life has been concentrated and is now made manifest in his features, the taut skin translucent over the serious brow.

Rhisiart sits by the bed and holds his dad's hand. He tells his dad all the things he needs to. He keeps it short. Suddenly Wiliam's eyes open. He smiles at his son and begins to sing, quietly but perfectly clearly.

Dal f'enaid i fynu, 'rwy'n ffaelu bob dydd,
A nertha fy nghalon yn ffyddlon mewn ffydd;
Rho imi dy Adnabod, yn Briod, yn frawd,
Yr ydwyf yn barod i'madael a'r cnawd.

Then Wiliam closes his eyes and his spirit is set free. For the next twenty minutes or so, they are all very still. When finally they move back from the bed, Rhisiart sees a prism of light above his dad, a rainbow of colour.

In death Wiliam looks regal, his other-worldly aspect filling Rhisiart with awe and a certain, natural dread. He looks like his dad, yet he doesn't look like his dad – he looks more impressive than his dad has done these last few months. He finds it impossible to put into words, but there is an aspect of both masculinity and femininity having been present. All duality, opposites, are no longer.

Nonconformist

LEGACY

Pentre Bwaau
1914

Rhisiart and Margaret hold religious services at Pentre
Bwaau for over forty years. Rhisiart's children and grand-
children are devout, building chapels in their communities, keeping Wiliam's spirit alive, and over the next century the independent chapels and schools flourish across
Wales, until there are nearly three thousand of them, with
an estimated figure of over one hundred and fifty thousand people having been taught in them.

Wiliam's descendants are so well-intentioned, but
as we tumble down through the generations, through the
births, deaths and marriages, they will fight over clocks,
cars, farms and wills.

In August 1914 Rhisiart's great-great-grandson Jack
comes out of the dark interior of Pentre Bwaau into the

bright day. Sheep are bleating, voices ring out, whistle commands. Someone is chopping wood, the sound of the axe overlaying the sheep in an odd rhythm. His nose streams, his eyes itch, he can feel them swell instantly as he cycles up the track to the clear road ahead. There is a war in France, and that is where he is going.

He signs up with the Royal Welsh Fusiliers on the 20th August, 1914. He tells them he is twenty, though he is just sixteen. He is stationed at Wrexham for training, then Conwy and Northampton.

In early November they are mobilised and land at Le Havre. In December they transfer to the 3rd Brigade of the 1st Division and see action on the Western Front, in Aubers and Loos. These small French towns surprise him in their sameness – they are not as exotically 'foreign' as he had imagined, the architecture and landscape not so far removed from his own homeland.

In October 1916 he is shot and sent back to a hospital in Shrewsbury and in November he is honourably discharged. He arrives back at Pentre with a metal plate in his leg and the Silver War Badge. At first the family are not quite sure how to treat him, they know something momentous has happened but don't know how to talk about it.

A generation of young men don't know how to talk about it, their high ideals of country, honour and glory lost along with their innocence, their brothers slaughtered in pointless battles. The fields around Pentre all look the same but everything else has changed.

Jack gets a job with the bank as an accountant and travels throughout Wales, living a bachelor life in Blaenau Ffestiniog and Barmouth before moving further south, to the border counties. In Llanidloes he meets Eileen, a dark-haired, pale-skinned French teacher, ambitious and lively. Her sister Gladys conducts the choir, her father is the postmaster in Cwmcarn and her mother is from a small mining village. Jack admires her, they marry and in 1934 John Bruce is born. They move up the country and have another son, Laurence, swiftly followed in 1940 by Julian, in Llandrindod Wells.

Now their first son Bruce is old enough, they send him to the local public school. After the first week Bruce pleads with his parents not to make him go – he is the only Welsh boy there – but Jack and Eileen insist. They argue about it, and though it is 'the done thing', Jack will never be entirely sure it is the right thing.

They move further north, to Shrewsbury, Colwyn Bay and finally Conwy, where Jack lands the manager's job, switching between Welsh and English, depending on the customer. Welsh is not spoken at home and the children are certainly not to learn it at the local school, swiftly removed from the Welsh to the French class. What little

Welsh the boys know is picked up from their grandparents and cousins when they visit Pentre Bwaau in the holidays. Eileen's ship is coming in, her ambitions know no bounds. She becomes captain of the Ladies golf team – Jack plays golf at the weekend and at any opportunity in between. He goes to chapel, while his wife does the flowers at church. He attends gala dinners and shakes hands. It nearly kills him. In fact, it does kill him, in the form of a painful and protracted cancer that ends his life age fifty-eight, in 1956.

Fairways

1970

Eileen's Trinity consists of St Johns, the golf club and bridge. She plants gladioli in the borders, and walks through the seaside town with a benign smile. Her dark *chignon* is smooth and tight, her buckled bag made of good leather. Older woman, sherbet lemon. Soft chin, hard nails. Aquiline nose, heavy brows above hooded eyes, bright as diamonds. Green tweed, fox stole.

She proffers her hand, nails ruby red.

'How do you do?'

The voice is lacquered – utterly, indisputably English. It is most certainly not the Cardiganshire accent of the village where her mother comes from. Eileen enunciates every vowel and consonant. She is the epitome of good manners, taking tea with her neighbours, the golf and church ladies. She collects the rent from Cadwgan Road and returns to Fairways, maintaining a regal pace up the hill.

Her house stands square behind the crenelated wall, the portico white against the red brick villa.she hangs the fox next to the mink, kicks off her shoes and makes her way through the house to the back room, where she sinks into the armchair with yesterday's *News of the World.*

Opaque smoke unfurls from her cigarette in its long holder as Winnie brings her a cuppa. Later she will go to the bingo with Gladys. Eileen can hear her son Julian, his wife and their daughter Rosamund Jane in the kitchen. They are talking to Winnie, there is the clatter of plates.

In the parlour, the occasional tables and three-piece suite are static, lit by the light of the bay window. Framed portraits of Jack and Eileen fix the room with their permanent gaze, husband and wife either side of the walnut bureau, the comfortable oils capturing them in their prime, painted when her skin was dewy, his hair fair.

Murano glass is arranged on polished wood, alongside the boxy silver cigarette case, available yet closed. Porcelain birds in primrose yellow and duck-egg blue perch on the mantelpiece in perpetual flight. The clock ticks.

Eileen will dote on Rosamund Jane, to some extent. The child has potential, standing still when Eilieen takes her shopping, twisting her wayward hair into tight curls, turning her full circle to critically assess her reflection.

Rosamund Jane will always act obediently, as a child. Easily overwhelmed, she is adept at containing strong emotions, so as not to disturb the grown-ups. Years later, she will ricochet between Threshers and Woolworths on Bangor highstreet. She is shouting, but does not know it.

The Blue Books

An old illustration depicts Wales as an ancient mother, her head as the island of Anglesey – Môn – in a black bonnet. It's a snug fit, a worn black hat, not the upright, uptight Victorian picture-postcard version. In similar vein, as though to fly in the face of tourist convention, this Mother Wales is no white-breasted Celtic maiden. She is a hag, a crone, her unkempt hair straggling to her lower jaw, the antithesis of chocolate-box kitsch.

The Llŷn Peninsula is her long arm, at the end of which rocky fingers grasp bewigged nineteenth century judges. She is dipping them into the sea – drowning them off the Cardigan coast. While the judges dangle and flail, wigs askew, upturned boots sinking in the dark waters off Mumbles, she is immovable, imperturbable. There is a sense of inevitability about this, for the judges at least. It is as though the old woman has, finally, had enough. *Mae hi 'di cael llond bol*: she has had

Dame Venodotia Sousing the Spies, Hugh Hughes, 1848

a bellyful. The judges appear tiny irritants, mere upstarts against her implacable body. This map of Mother Wales was a visual response to the damning government reports on education in Wales at the time. These 'Blue Books' as they became known, provoked outrage amongst the indigenous Welsh, not least for the inflammatory language in which the report's English authors presented contemporary Wales – a series of biased accounts which depicted Wales and the Welsh as poor and ignorant. More, that the laziness and immorality was in large part due to the Welsh language and nonconformism to the Anglican church.

Although in the illustration old Mother Wales easily disposes of the hapless judges, in reality the authority and influence of the English commissioners was less easy to dispel.

In describing the Welsh language as 'a great evil', the Report promulgated the supremacy of English. This inevitably provoked hostility – put less politely, the Welsh felt as though they had been shafted, and not for the first time.

It is an insidious thing, a clever and cruel thing, to convince a culture of its own inferiority. It inculcates a feeling of shame, of guilt, in using a mother tongue, so that you turn yourself inside out to try to escape it. The cultural erosion was centuries long and systematic.

The history of Wales is tumultuous, with a merging of fact and fiction involving warrior princes, sea-striding giants and raven-haired princesses. A line of incanting Druids momentarily paralyse the Roman invasion at the Menai Strait. Saints – lots of them – set off from Ireland. Bobbing in coracles, these tiny vessels circle on the cold sea, caught in the eddies and flows around Ynys Enlli, precarious above the fathomless deep. They settle in cells, talk to curlews.

Long after the Romans and saints, around the thirteenth century, English castles pop up – strongholds altogether more rectangular, less transient than any coracle. The native people retreat to the interior, to the mountains and inaccessible places, the island and long arm of the Llŷn. Like snow thawing on mountains, as R.S. Thomas would have it – 'always in retreat'. Some years the snow is visible even in June, the jagged white lines deep in the crevasses of the Carneddau – *esgyrn eira*.

Llanddaniel Fab
2016

We move from Tyn Llan to the village of Llanddaniel Fab. The music of the ice cream van warbles in the mid-afternoon. There are pots on the kitchen windowsill. Dogs bark, buses rumble and sometimes it reminds me of a glorious summer suburbia, even though it is only March. The blackbird thinks I am planting just for him.

There are four roads leading out of this village, one of which runs past Bodlewfawr. I have seen the farm marked on maps and from my cycle rides reckon it's the tall dark house set back from the road.

In this main room I can see the half-moon through the square roof light, two windows pour the daylight in. The stove roars with thick early flames of coals. The light is captured, still in this central space. The blue hour. The sky is the colour of sugared violets, a pale gradient to the horizon.

I go to Nant Gwrtheyrn on a residential course, past the tinderstick tree trunks on the abandoned mountainside, down the gorge to the National Welsh Language Centre. I stay there for three days in my own underfloor-heated terrace house. I can't sleep for the words in my head, and have to write them down.The emphasis has changed from English to Welsh in my inner voice, which is full of words from the day – sentences, mutations and so on. Some of these words – their form, shape and colour, are like jewels in my mouth. I'm wondering about the power of it and whether the force of a language that skips one generation carries on to the next. It's very tiring, because each word is a new word, every sound a new sound. Nothing is the same – everything is different.

The bed is quiet, a little cold, but there is a Welsh wool blanket on it and socks on my feet. There is only the darkness outside, the mountains above and the sea quietly close. There is such stillness in this place, it allows things to remain and to be. The stillness allows thought to happen, without fear of fine timetables or tired day.

A couple of weeks after I get home from Nant Gwrtheyrn I drive down to the Menai Strait, where the wind makes choppy waves in the narrow channel. All the little houses of Y Felinheli line up on the other side, rising up the high bank, the sun reflected from their windows. The cows are a smart black and white against the greenest grass in the field next to Pilot Cottage.

Moel y Don is a smooth white house right on the water's edge, where I walk down the concrete jetty that runs into the sound. Just along from this is the stone and metal of an older pier and preserved in the mud is the skeleton of a large boat – a barge perhaps – roughly thirty foot long by ten foot wide.

Last week there was a referendum in Britain, on whether to remain in the European Union, or to leave. When I got up on Friday morning the first words my daughter said to me were,

'We are out of Europe and the Prime Minister has resigned'.

In June just over half the country voted Out, and just under half voted In. There is a constitutional crisis, a deep sense of shock, because nobody, not even the Leave voters, expected this to happen. There is a palpable sense of unease. It's felt that the Leave argument was fuelled by right wing anti-immigration sentiment in the press. It's said that some used the Leave choice as a protest vote, fed up with large corporate power. It feels very divisive.

'It's not good on the streets. One half of the country think the other half are wankers' a friend writes on social media.

The pound has plummeted, stock market graphs show peaks and deep troughs in alarming red lines. The Governor of the Bank of England is poised to pump two hundred and fifty billion pounds into the economy. Quantitative easing, it's called. There is a picture of him, a Canadian saviour, backed by a plaque and flanked by microphones on his podium. Nobody has ever seen anything like it. Nobody knows what is going to happen.

Both mainstream political parties are being ripped apart internally by resignations and votes of no confidence. The young voters (who mostly voted Remain) are taking to the streets with messages of 'We Love EU' on big placards as they swarm into Parliament Square.

Racist incidents have increased since the result. 'Britain is Not a Rainswept Racist Island' the rather desperate headline of one broadsheet article. There is a 'leadership vacuum'. In Scotland, a statesmanlike Nicola Sturgeon puts Scottish independence 'very much on the table'. There is a rally for an Independent Wales in Caernarfon.

I love the smells of summer – of old coffee and trapped sunshine, fired clay dust. On the salty Menai Strait this morning salmon pink strips of sand stretch out, making it possible, surely, to simply walk across to Caernarfon. There is a narrow channel of reflected light, but it must be just a few strides, if you walk it quickly.

Archive
2017

On dull days I find myself picking up the yellow book – the book Maxie gave me. Written in deep Welsh, it is an account of Wiliam Prichard and the Independent movement, written by Dafydd Wyn Wiliam, a minister of religion. It is as though there is no option but to learn the language enough to decipher this thing. I seem to hope that the more I read it the more I will understand, until eventually I am fluent. It is a very slow, laborious process.

At Bangor University Library Archive, no pens are allowed. We write in pencil and to facilitate this there are very nifty upright pencil sharpeners. The archivist and I rifle through the index cards. There are loads of John Williamses and then there he is – *Prichard, Wiliam, Cnwchdernog.*

The manuscripts, when they are brought up, are bound in hardback folios. The pages look like mottled, ancient maps, with some evidence of restoration – I can see how fresh paper has been adhered to the frayed edges, to secure the pages safely within the spine.

When I explain what I am doing to the archivist, she mentions that Dafydd Wyn Wiliam, the author of the yellow book, is in the archive most Mondays. So the next Monday morning I am back in the archive, trying to be nonchalant but actually quite shy.

Dafydd Wyn Wiliam is there when I arrive, his tweed trilby resting on top of the catalogue index. He is deep in study and occasional conversation with another man sitting opposite him. I don't want to disturb them, so I take my time and wait for a natural opening.

When I introduce myself and explain my interest in Wiliam and the yellow book, immediately Dafydd Wyn Wiliam refers to Moses – the King, the Prophet.

'Wiliam was not afraid of anybody except his God,' he says.

The questions I ask are unplanned. My aim is to be coherent, to stick to simple Welsh so as not to trip over myself.

'Are there any pictures of Wiliam?' I ask.

'No,' he shakes his head. 'In those days it would have been a painting. But, you know,' he smiles at me, 'as you belong to Wiliam, something of him will be in you.'

Dafydd Wyn Wiliam was the first to go down to London and look in the archives there to see the court cases brought against Wiliam Prichard. I have to focus hard to follow the complex vocabulary as he tells me that the London Dissenters were an influential body who helped Wiliam financially and legally.

'It would have been a different story without their support,' he says.

I manage to keep my language Welsh throughout our short talk.

'Are you coming to the Eisteddfod?' he asks. 'Come and see us in the 'Morisiaid' tent. Maxie was a member.'

I say I am and I will.

He says he is glad I am researching my background. His eyes are as clear as can be, and his handshake warm. I thank him, and settle down to the day's batch of manuscripts which the archivist has laid out for me.

I photograph the fore-edges of the papers as they lie one on top of the other in a sheaf. The content, colours and texture combined – there is something about this that resonates deep inside me, a visceral gurgle of joy, in the specificity of the original writing and the ubiquity of the old pages. I love it in the same way I love the shiny tobacco colours of the 1940s Sellotape that holds the pages together.

Acts of Union
2017

In July, at the end of the academic year, we sit in the lecture hall for the CEO's annual address. After the presentation about this year's achievements – the profits rounded up into halves of millions, we are to remain seated for a presentation from a company that is going to deliver the proposed new power station on the island.

In the presentation we are guided through the make and model of the state of the art nuclear power station that will be sited at Cemlyn, by the bird sanctuary. We are shown some overhead plans of the site, the blue rectangles are the offices and residential quarters. This is Phase 1 of the project, they will be seeking planning approval to build roads and move hills for Phase 2.

We are told the timescale of the project, the different

phases, the many jobs it will create. It is a very detailed presentation by a customer relations guy. He is very thorough but it's getting on towards lunchtime and you can feel people beginning to shuffle in their seats.

The PR guy is running through some final Key Information, about how the power station building is designed in order to be de-commissioned – built to last a hundred years or so. He is gliding through bullet points – something scientific about geological distribution. Somebody's hand slowly goes up in the air, before I realise with horror that it is mine.

'*Yes!*'

PR Guy spots me and turns a bright smile in my direction.

'I apologise for my lack of understanding, but I wonder if I could ask a question?'

He is nodding encouragingly. I doubt my colleagues are as enthused as he is.

'I notice a couple of slides ago the phrase *geological distribution*. I wonder if you could tell me what that means please?'

'Yes, it's rather a fancy scientific name, isn't it! Essentially it means that the nuclear waste is secured underground within the rock, as a nuclear dump.'

I wonder if the rest of the audience are as surprised as I am that he has just introduced the term *nuclear dump*.

It's not a phrase he has used in the presentation up until now. He goes on to tell us just exactly how the cases containing the nuclear waste are made secure, looking me directly in the eye as I am drawn into a world of casings and castings, lead and concrete, as though this were a Roni Horn seminar.

The casings have to be highly secure because they have to last *for ever*, as nuclear waste is highly radioactive and does not decompose.

I appreciate his attention to detail and am encouraged to follow up.

'How much space does it take up underground – are you talking about half an acre?'

'Yes – something like that. I think it was measured in swimming pools, or buses. Can you remember?'

PR guy calls out to tech support at the back of the room.

'Eighteen double-decker buses,'

Tech support calls back, heard but unseen.

'Yes, that's it. Eighteen double-decker buses, or about five Olympic-size swimming pools. That gives you an idea of the scale of it.'

It's become so conversational I feel able to continue with another question.

'And would the waste be stored underneath the power plant itself, or transported elsewhere?'

I imagine radioactive lorries hurtling up the A55 and so I miss the first part of his answer, I just catch the ending – 'They are looking for volunteer communities to come forward.'

There is a spontaneous ripple of laughter from the audience. PR Guy is slightly disconcerted by this, as though we doubt him.

'Yes,' he assures us, 'a community in Cumbria have shown an interest.'

The rising volume in the audience has nothing to do with lunch.

'It's much less now though than it used to be, isn't it?' a voice next to me pipes up.

'The waste – it's much less now than it used to be.'

It's the woman from Marketing.

A couple of weeks later on a Saturday afternoon I am heading home with the shopping when I get a text from cousin Joel: *'do you want to come to an exhibition in Newborough'*.

I turn out of Home Bargains Llangefni as the next text beeps – *'today'*.

As I am working out the logistics of how to do this, I find I am passing the signpost to Newborough, so I take it, in an act of spontaneity which will delay the fish pie by about six hours. The road through Llangaffo dips, bends and very shortly I reach the village.

'In JP Institute' the next text reads.

I don't know what the exhibition is about, but the 'FUKUSHIMA – WALES' AA signs give me an idea. As I walk into the hall there are guys walking around in T-shirts bearing the words WYLFASHIMA underneath a nuclear 'Munch' scream.

The show is a visual documentary of life in the six years after the nuclear reactor blew up in the province of Fukushima, Japan. There is a room of photographs and an adjoining audio-visual installation, which Joel has edited. He and I sit in this darkened room and watch the video.

It is footage of a landscape, seen from the vantage point of the driver of a bus as it makes its way through towns and villages. It could be anywhere – at first I think it is Dwygyfylchi or Gaerwen – but in the next sequence a tidal wave decimates a town, in real time, the water destroying everything effortlessly.

'Is that the tsunami?' I whisper.

'Yes,' Joel whispers back.

The water is magnificently black as it rushes from the left to the right of the frame.

'We don't have tsunamis in the Irish Sea.' I lean over again.

'No. We have earthquakes though. Shh. Watch the film.'

The video is a montage of newsreel and the artist's footage of travelling into the contaminated region, the Geiger counter on the dashboard of the bus fluctuating erratically. The houses are low-level, the vegetation overgrown. The buildings are unoccupied, abandoned.

The video is slow, the soundtrack throbbing and sinister, pulsating. We see the reactor explode in slow motion, and as the plume of smoke rises into the air we are aware that some poison is being released into the atmosphere, irrevocably. The imagery begins to saturate – repetitive scenes of utter destruction. Views of abundant pink blossom on a tree-lined avenue are accompanied by the knowledge that this beauty is purely superficial, that a malignant chemistry has become embedded in the structure.

As details are enlarged, the images become increasingly abstract. Biological cells are bound by grids of ever expanding networks which encompass everything – landscape, people – nothing can escape the toxicity once it is released into the air. Rain, clouds, leaves, bones, cells – radiation is absorbed into everything, causing cancers, disfigurements and untold misery.

There is a poignant voice-to-camera piece by a Japanese woman reading in English.

'I so much enjoyed visiting Wales,' she says, 'the wide green landscape of Anglesey – this memory will stay with me forever.'

She is one of the delegation who came here, compelled to warn against the building of the proposed new nuclear reactors on the island.

'We understand how people think it will benefit the community – create jobs, boost the economy, keep the young people from moving away. This is what we thought,' she says.

'But look at us. Fifty years after the building of it and one hundred and twenty thousand of us are refugees, unable to return to our homes because it is too dangerous. I believe humans can learn from their mistakes. Please, learn from our mistake.'

As she finishes talking the screen is taken up with a computer-generated three-dimensional model of the proposed new nuclear site – a digital visualisation of a flattened, 360° view which shows the huge grey windowless structures within the landscape.

The coast around Cemaes and the inlets beyond – Rhoscolyn and Rhosneigr are in the upper part of the frame. The sea is shining, a naturalised glare off the water. It looks so pretty, that part of the picture, in its enhanced virtual form, that you can't help but wonder at the absurdity of this proposal at all.

The voiceovers, deliberately amalgamated to start in Welsh and run into English finish with the line 'no moral justification' and you have to think that is the case.

We leave the darkened room and go to the tea room downstairs, where I am introduced to the artist, a doctor, his wife and a couple of guys wearing those 'WYLFASH-IMA' T-shirts. We talk over tea and cake, about what this proposal means to the island.

'I know I am romantic,' I say.

'I have come to accept that in myself. I don't know about the technical aspects of energy, but I can't help thinking that Anglesey could be so much more *without* this power station.'

Part of my coming to appreciate Welsh, when we lived in Tyn Llan, is that it was 'other'. It was, by definition, not English, and all that larger global language represents. It seems to me that it is this very 'otherness' that makes the Welsh language unique. I feel I have to be careful somewhere inside, that there is a danger of my talking 'about' Welsh, from the outside – that is, as an English person articulating something of 'what it is'. One way I have found to mitigate this is not to talk 'about' Welsh, but to speak it, where I can, even though my vocabulary is limited.

'To my mind, in the twenty-first-century world, with its incessant, increasing anxiety, consumption and depression, Anglesey's role could be one of 'otherness', of healing and peace,' I say.

The coastal path, on which the new reactor is to be

built, is an Area of Outstanding Natural Beauty, used to market the island as a tourist destination. So how would it be if Anglesey became a leading community in the development of an alternative approach to energy, housing and jobs? Already cutting-edge industries are investing in renewable energy sources such as tidal power here. Tidal and solar, environmentally-astute new-build houses would invest a quality and integrity into island people's lives which could be an *attraction* to visitors.

People come and go over cups of tea around the table as we talk. The conversation turns to the fragility of the system, ecologically and in terms of the Welsh language.

The doctor says, quite calmly, that larger languages have always overrun minority languages. A farmer and his wife from Amlwch, not far from the site of the new-build reactor discuss their views. He is for it – but only just.

'Jobs for the young, isn't it,' he shrugs resignedly.

His wife, on the other hand, is not in favour at all.

'It will destroy the language,' she says.

'Imagine all those people coming in – they don't want to learn the language. No, in another fifty years, it will be gone.'

So there is this fine balance, a delicate ecosystem that needs to be tended, attended to in order to develop opportunity and growth.

As for nuclear, if the Japanese government is banning new-build nuclear in its own country, why on earth would we want to do it here?

I am leaning over the table talking to the doctor, about the history of the Welsh language, the 1536 Act of Union, where Wales was legally incorporated into England, and the language clause, meaning English became Wales' sole official language.

'The language was to be *expurgated*,' he laughs gently, stirring his tea.

'You don't hear that word very often.'

We talk a bit about where we come from, our origins.

'Here's something to keep in the back of your mind,' he says.

'If a couple of English people meet abroad, one of the first things they will ask each other is "what do you do?" If a couple of Welsh people meet each other abroad, one of the first things they ask is — '

'Where are you from?' I interject.

He points at me and nods. I think about how pleased I was when somebody referred to me as 'Jane Tyn Llan'.

As we're talking a woman with long blonde hair sits herself down between us, at the head of the small table.

'Oh!' she says abruptly, 'you're talking Welsh. I'll leave then.' And she makes to stand up.

'Oh no, there's no need!' I say, a little taken aback.

'We can talk in English just as well.'

So we switch languages, to be polite.

'We were talking about the Act of Union, about how the law in Wales had to be in English only,' I say.

'Did it?' she says 'I didn't know. Was it in Welsh before that, then? When was that?'

The doctor explains and she questions him, drawing on his wealth of knowledge.

'I had no idea that the things we see today – road signage, bilingual signage, had to be fought for, politically in the seventies – I just took it for granted that it had always been this way.' I say.

'But the road signs have always been in Welsh, haven't they?' the woman frowns.

The doctor explains that no, this is not the case, that there has not always been parity between the two languages.

'Where do you live?' the doctor asks her.

She pronounces the town's name in a way so unlike its original form that I feel a bit embarrassed for her. I have done this myself, I remind myself – mispronounced French place names terribly when we lived there. She has lived in this town for twenty-five years. Her children are all bilingual.

'Two of them took to it, but my son's spelling was bad, at school. He would put in the wrong letters.'

I nod, understandingly. I noticed that in my own kids' spelling, for a time, but thought it a small price to pay for them being able to speak the language.

The doctor explains a 'transition' period with children, in learning two languages simultaneously.

'They learn so quickly, children,' she says, 'like sponges. It's more difficult when you're older.'

She shakes her head glumly. 'You've got to be brainy, to learn a language.'

I shake my head back.

'I disagree. I don't think it's braininess. I think it's desire, commitment.'

She looks at me dolefully and I realise I am not interested in the energy it takes to convince.

The day eventually breaks up and I drive the back roads home, put together the fish pie. It is much later when I am driving north to Pencarnisiog on a teenage taxi run, the sky a slow red above the A55, in the distance the shine of the sea around Rhoscolyn and Holy Island. I think of the revellers at the National Eisteddfod in Bodedern, just a few miles inland.

Eisteddfod
2017

Through some digging about on the internet I find that all my unformed ideas of a non-nuclear future for the island have already been written about. The 'Manifesto for Môn' outlines an economic development strategy for the island, addressing demography, employment, the nuclear industry and the island's resources in turn. There are guidelines for job creation – in energy conservation, wind, solar, biomass, sea and geothermal.

The manifesto's guidelines on jobs growth – in tourism, ICT and healthy food production give a projected figure of nearly three thousand jobs over a twenty year restructuring period. Germany wants to be shot of nuclear energy by 2020, which begs the question – why is the UK pushing nuclear ahead?

I am wondering about these things on Sunday morning as I cut out two dozen pastry circles and realise my counting is in Welsh, in my head.

On Wednesday night I go to an Eisteddfod event at a posh hotel. The reception is full of piano music, prosecco and hors d'oeuvres – the menu is an artform in itself. I speak Welsh all evening and when I arrive home I am buzzing. I stick the telly on to unwind and see there is a debate on Newsnight about new legislation regarding Wales. 'Welsh language – Help or Hindrance?' is the feature's title.

The 'debate' is between two contributors, neither of whom speak the language, one of whom slams the cost of English to Welsh translation services as taking money from the NHS. It is cobblers and I say as much on Twitter, which is awash – an awoken dragon – with complaints about the slant of the piece. So when I go to bed my brain is popping with *that*, but more, it is thinking about it *in Welsh*. Which prompts the English part of my brain to try to reassert itself, provoking an intense, dualistic internal dialogue, around 1 a.m.

I remember feeling a bit like this after a night out in Brittany with the neighbours, in full-on French. The next day we would be 'French fried', having spent hours trying to decipher words, sentences and phrases of the native speakers, the internal translation and response. The feeling hits you *after* the event – it is as though there are slightly too many electrical currents going on in the brain, the sheer concentration of having to think that bit harder before you speak, having to reach for a vocabulary of new words, storing some in deep memory, keeping some on the easily-accessible shelf – a cognitively complex process which leaves my brain fizzing.

The next day I go to the Eisteddfod for the first time. It's huge. Huge and hot and dry, full of bookstalls and peace stalls and music and dance. The ground is spongy where it has rained like fury and then been baked by the sun. I take a back seat in a circular yurt – Tŷ Gwerin – and listen to five harpists. I hang out in Manon's Art place and eat my lunch outside on a pink beanbag, watching the kids and couples, babies, teenagers, artists and performers.

I give a short speech at an event to celebrate the winner of the 'Learner of the Year' competition. The archdruid happens to be in the crowd and there is an impromptu ceremony, where he holds a homespun crown aloft.

'*A oes heddwch?*' he shouts.

'*Heddwch!*' the crowd cheer back. Peace. He places the crown on her head.

With the tea and cake I get talking to Siân, my old Welsh tutor. She tells me about the strategic wardrobe decisions you have to make, living in a caravan for a week on the Eisteddfod field.

On the bus back home the conversation is louder, more relaxed, in Welsh and English. I think – any Newsnight reporters ought to witness this, in order to answer their own question.

In the wake of the car crash of the Newsnight interview there is a petition for an independent review into how the BBC portrays the Welsh language. The next edition of Newsnight features a sort of apology – they 'recognise that a lot of people think there should have been a Welsh speaker involved in the debate'.

The presenter tells us that English-speaking Welsh people 'are representative of Wales' and that the programme would also have liked a Welsh speaker to have been present. They play out with footage from the Welsh rock band *Yr Eira* from that day's Eisteddfod.

I don't know whether it's because I'm sensitised to this, reading as I am about Welsh history and 'identity', but suddenly there seems to be a lot of this sort of thing about. There was the 'Ring of Iron' a few weeks ago – an heritage proposed public sculpture, which celebrated the castles within the country as part of Wales' 'Year of Legends'. People objected to these representations of English rule being celebrated in such a way and that project is being re-thought pretty quickly. I can't help wondering about the same organisation's Twitter stream too – their marketing targeted at parents entertaining their kids in the summer holidays. Beneath colour shots of military re-en-actments from the Middle Ages within these castles the caption reads 'Whose side are you on?'

Shortly after the 'Ring of Iron' debacle, Bangor's branch of a national sports shop forbid their workers to speak Welsh to one another. This is apparently because non-Welsh speakers are unable to understand them. There is a public outcry. There is a lot of support for the Welsh language from Welsh people who do not speak it – that's the majority of people in Wales, although it doesn't feel like it from where I've been standing the last few days.

I have to stop my finger becoming Twitter-trig-ger-happy when I see the nuclear power company's posts. Their astonishing purple logo is on the backdrop of a computer-generated visualisation of the site – the same idealised 3D virtual world we saw in the Fukushima film, the lapping waves of the Irish Sea top of the frame – this is their Twitter masthead.

There is a post from the local county show, with a photograph of a giant blue robot 'boy' and giant pink robot 'girl' – cartoonish and larger-than-life – standing beside a human boy and girl. The cap-tion 'A warm welcome at the show!' is not ironic. 'A damn sight warmer if your radiation leaks' I almost write – but don't, because I am a coward and I'm not sure whether it serves any purpose.

There is another post, a shot of a group of the company's staff at the show, grinning and waving in a never-ending ten-second GIF. In another post there is an advert for job opportunities, one of which is for an Emergency Manager. The role involves *Developing policies and strategies that define the company's approach to emergency planning for conventional and radiation emergencies.* Good luck with that then.

Porth Nobla

2019

The further back we go, the deeper we reach. There is a relationship between the conscious and the unconscious, what we 'know' to what we 'know, but don't know we know'.

The thread to an ancient past provides connections that resonate – aspects of our ancestors that we may not consciously know about find a way of expressing them-selves in our contemporary lives – you could call it our spiritual DNA.

I'm sitting at the computer, ostensibly doing some work but actually reading about Welsh History. It's funny, I remember learning about World War II in History class, but nothing about Welsh history. This omission seems a bit odd, given that we were sitting in the shadow of

Harlech Castle, but may have been because I was down by the river smoking fags with Tracey.

Now I'm reading about the history of the Welsh language, learning about the distinct strands of 'Celtic' and 'Germanic' as different cultures. I understand myself as a product of a merging between the two – I have more Celtic strands in me than Germanic, I think.

At college in Liverpool I could 'do' Welsh, and enjoyed the difference it gave me. The first two lines of the national anthem was enough to cause a stir, a party trick to pull out after the third pint of Guinness.

I knew Welsh as a novelty – nothing really serious. In Wales, I could hear my English friends fill the void in Blaenau pubs, as all eyes turn to stare. If you are eighteen and a hippy, with saggy jumpers and raggedy mates, they'll just about let you off.

I have often thought of myself as somewhere in between, not quite one thing nor the other. Sometimes when I felt deeply, and searched for the right words, those that surfaced surprised me – odd, archaic words, like *gwddf* and *fy nghalon*.

I understand something more about the dichotomy or duality within myself now – sometimes I have felt neither fully one thing (English) nor the other (Welsh). That is, neither fully one thing (Welsh) nor the other (English). It can feel a little like no-man's land, if you are having a not-so-confident day – seen from another perspective, it is an empowering place, being able to bridge two cultures and languages.

I am working on a freelance job where my colleague keeps in touch using a combination of formal Welsh and totally made-up Wenglish words. It's great: I love it. I am learning different words much faster now, and know the difference between presentation (*cyflwyniad*), interview (*cyfweliad*) and audience (*cynulleidfa*). When I am speaking Welsh, if I am tired my brain still stalls, but on the whole it's getting better.

Cymraeg is an ancient language, going back four thousand years, compared with English, which goes back about fifteen hundred years. It has its origins in Celtic, an Indo-European language which was around six thousand years ago. The Celts may have been the first Indo-European people to spread across Europe – to Germany, Spain, Italy and Britain. Place names such as London, Paris, Rhone and Danube are Celtic in origin.

The Brythonic language is a Celtic language, from which Cymraeg, Cumbrian and Cornish are direct descendants. Brythonic was spoken throughout the whole of this island until the Romans invaded, when Latin was the language of administration. Brythonic continued to be spoken by most of the population and, when the Romans left, the Brythonic language reasserted itself.

Brythonic was understood the length and breadth of the country, and our Welsh language now is derived from the Brythonic source, with adaptations from Irish and Latin in the mix.

'Gwynedd' and 'Llŷn' – words I recognise as distinctly Welsh – are actually derived from Irish, widely spoken in Wales for a couple of centuries after the Romans left. The Welsh word for rag –'*cadach*' – is Irish, and '*eglwys*' – church – is from Latin.

Similarly, many familiar English words are Welsh in origin – 'Avon' is derived from the Welsh word for river: '*afon*'. Discovering these links makes me smile, as it shows there is no pure strain of any one thing – that there has always been this flux and amalgamation, this interplay between languages and cultures, a rise and fall of power. Landscape and language are inextricably linked.

This ancient land, where Brythonic would have been understood across the country, was carved up into England, Scotland, Wales and Cornwall. While the Irish and Scottish influx into Wales was going on in the north-west, down in the south-east there was another invasion happening, from Germany and the Netherlands.

In effect, the Anglo-Saxons took over where the Romans left off, moving up the country to the river Severn, colonising communities on their way. They spoke Old English and as they advanced north they called the indigenous Brythonic speakers 'Wealas' or 'Welsh', which can be translated as 'foreigner'. To describe *themselves* the Welsh used the name *Cymry* – a name derived from Brythonic meaning 'fellow-countryman'.

I turn the computer off and drive to the beach. I reflect on the idea of *disallowing* a language – such a conscious decision – nothing arbitrary about it.

'We're moving to Prestatyn and we're not speaking Welsh anymore' – a friend told me of her own family's experience – how common this experience was.

I wonder whether this disallowing caused a chasm, a rift in our cultural heritage, a rip between the old world and the new, and wonder about the inner convulsion it takes to conform. Perhaps social success came with hidden costs, buried not far beneath the surface, a terrible, introverted pain. It feels like a violent act.

At Porth Nobla the tide is neither in nor out. It is on the turn, and for a moment there is this delicious equanimity. I lie in the shallows where the water meets the sand and let the waves run over me, a dreamy silken in and out, a liquid breathing.

The pellucid water shows each individual pebble and rock clearly defined in their blues, reds and yellow ochres. Fans of seaweed sway, their tendrils lazily follow the slow swell. It is as warm as bathwater as I swim through the surface to the outcrop of rocks which form a small island.

The water is as blue as the sky – there is no difference at all, the landscape of the one giving up to the landscape of the other. I stand on the island and look back, into the sun. There is nobody else on the beach but a cormorant on the black rocks behind me. I wade in again and swim back to shore, the salt water a glaze. I pad up the sand on flat feet to the line of marram grass and lie back, to gaze out at the sea through half-closed eyes.

The sunlight creates lozenges of glare which shimmer, but give no indication of motion, even though the tide must be pulling the water in and out. On the surface there is this horizontal shift and dazzle, but no sense of the water coming closer or receding.

Jane Parry is a fine artist, educator, book designer and author. She studied Fine Art at Liverpool before postgraduate studies in Printing and Publishing and then Contemporary Art in London. This is her second novel, after the memoir *Lessons in Impermanence* which chronicled her family's temporary move to France. She lives with her husband in North Wales.

Published work

Downstream, Tales from the Pandemic, Awyr Las 2022

The New Welsh Curriculum, Wales Arts Review 2018

Fukushima – Cymru: Science meets Art in an Exposé of Nuclear Meltdown, lisfields.org 2017

Lessons in Impermanence, Parthian Books 2014

Book Design – Principles and Process, OCA 2012

www.janeparry.co.uk

Printed in Great Britain
by Amazon